DEATH WISH

Books by Angela Roquet

Lana Harvey, Reapers Inc.
Graveyard Shift
Pocket Full of Posies
For the Birds
Psychopomp
Death Wish
Ghost Market
Hellfire and Brimstone
Limbo City Lights (short story collection)
The Illustrated Guide to Limbo City

Return to Limbo City (A Lana Harvey Spin-off Series)
Life After Death
Shadow of Death

Blood Vice
Blood Vice
Blood and Thunder
Blood in the Water
Blood Dolls
Thicker Than Blood
Blood, Sweat, and Tears
Flesh and Blood
Out for Blood

Spero Heights
Blood Moon
Death at First Sight
The Midnight District

Haunted Properties: Magic and Mayhem Universe
How to Sell a Haunted House
Better Haunts and Graveyards
This Old Haunt

Visit **angelaroquet.com** for a complete list of Angela's works.

LANA HARVEY, REAPERS INC.

BOOK FIVE

ANGELA ROQUET

VIOLENT SIREN PRESS

DEATH WISH

Copyright © 2015 by Angela Roquet

This is a work of fiction. Names, characters, places, and incidents either are the product of the author's imagination or are used fictitiously. Any resemblance to actual events or locales or persons, living or dead, is entirely coincidental.

www.angelaroquet.com

Cover Art by Rebecca Frank

Edited by Chelle Olson of Literally Addicted to Detail

ISBN: 978-1-951603-04-5

For George Shelley,
THE professor.

Thank you for keeping an eye on Lana. She'd probably
be aimlessly wandering around Limbo City without
your encouragement and insight these past few years.

CHAPTER ONE

*"Democracy is the art and science of running the circus
from the monkey cage."*
—H. L. Mencken

I'd never harvested anyone from a circus before. I really didn't see what all the hype was about, but that could have been because I missed the main act. And seeing as how the second act went up in flames—the reason I was there in the first place—I didn't even have time to enjoy a quick bag of popcorn.

The fire had already reached the concession stand, and the plastic popper box melted around the blackened kernels inside, mixing with the gamey smell of elephant crap. And people actually *paid* for this?

My stomach grumbled, reminding me that I'd missed lunch, and I cursed Kevin again. My no-show apprentice was in for an earful when I caught up with him. Picking up his slack was starting to weigh on me, and I'd been coddling him long enough. Still, I was having trouble coming right out and saying what needed to be said.

It wasn't as if I didn't miss Josie, too. We all did. Losing her had been a crippling blow, and no one was dealing with it particularly well. Gabriel was in full-on weeping angel mode,

Jenni had buried herself in work and avoided the subject altogether, and Kevin seemed to think he was going to find Josie hiding out in the bottom of a bottle.

I wasn't doing so great myself, but at least I could hold my liquor and make it to work on time. My anger issues were another story. Between Josie's death and Beelzebub's betrayal, my fuse was short and frayed. The fact that Bub was a double agent for our side of the war didn't ease my mind enough to count, but that might have something to do with the demon defense course he dropped in my lap when he took off without an explanation. Running the Posy Unit and taking on massive harvests without my apprentice was catching up with me, too.

Under the flaming big top, a mob of performers and attendees crowded the exits. Some tore at the heavy canvas, trying to find another way out as the tent filled with smoke. The amateur fire dancer who had sparked the emergency situation lay in the center ring, well-done. The girl was at the top of my harvest list, and I needed to take her soul before the tent collapsed unless I wanted to mar my perfect record by reporting her CNH, *currently not harvestable.*

The rest of the victims would be reachable along the outer rim and just beyond the fallen tent. If Kevin had met me as we planned, this harvest would have been easy-peasy. Instead, I was trying to decide which exit would yield the most casualties since I would undoubtedly be sprinting from one side to the other as souls prematurely fled their bodies. Trauma is a bitch like that. And, let me tell you, harvesting souls from a fire is no easy feat. Too much of the time, they freak out and think they're in Hell. I was going to *kill* Kevin for making me pull this job off alone.

A flaming beam broke loose from the tent's center pole, and I leapt over the edge of the risers just in time. I landed hard and twisted my ankle before falling face-first onto the dirt floor. Splintered wood and embers flew over me. I covered my head with my arms and scooted away, closer to the center ring.

The fire dancer's soul quivered under her skin, briefly poking through as she struggled to free herself. Her death was the most traumatic, which was why she needed to be harvested right away. If not, she would likely leave her body unassisted and wander. If she was lucky, someone from the Lost Souls Unit would pick her up quickly. If she was unlucky, she could end up roaming the Earth for years—decades even—reliving her death until a reaper stumbled across her.

I didn't need that on my conscience. I stood, tested out my sore ankle, and then hurried to the girl's side. Her charred flesh was rough like tree bark, but when my hand clasped around the wrist of her spectral form, she felt cool and smooth. She sprang out of her body with a scream.

"Quiet," I hissed. My patience was thin, and I didn't have time to comfort her, not if I wanted to collect the rest of the souls on my docket.

The girl's eyes swelled as she took in the flaming scene around us. "Am I dead? Is this Hell?"

"Slow down. You're getting ahead of yourself," I said, taking a small clipboard from the pocket of my robe.

"Oh my God. This *is* Hell. Isn't it?" She put her hands over her mouth and choked out a strangled sound.

I scanned the names on my list of souls. "Look, Bryony—"

"Brandy," she said. "I'm Brandy. My *sister* is Bryony. So maybe you have the wrong girl? Maybe my sister is actually supposed to be in Hell, and I'm not?"

I groaned and thrust my finger at the charred remains behind her. "That is your body. You are dead. This is not Hell. It's a circus, or what's left of a circus, that you've successfully sabotaged. Congratulations. Now, where do you suppose I might find this sister of yours?"

Brandy looked around more carefully, squinting through the smoke at the tightrope and the abandoned clown car nearby. Her cheeks flushed, and she twisted her fingers together over her chest. I had to snap *my* fingers in her face to regain her attention.

"Your sister?" I asked again.

"She's sleeping in her trailer, just outside. I wanted to fill in for her tonight," she said hollowly.

I sighed. "Great. So she'll probably wake up and make it out of this mess, and I can turn you in instead."

Brandy's face darkened. "I drugged her."

"What?"

"I *really* wanted to be in the show."

I rubbed my forehead. "You've got to be kidding me."

Visions of Kevin scrubbing the deck floor with a toothbrush filled my mind but were soon pushed away as another soul zipped into my line of sight and threw a solid right hook into Brandy's face.

"You stupid bitch," the new soul roared. The specter's face was twisted with rage, but despite that, she looked almost identical to Brandy. My mood lifted a little as I watched the two sisters pull hair and slap at each other.

"Your show was lame anyway!" Brandy squealed.

"*This* is why I never lit the hoops, you dimwit," her sister said, ripping the sleeve of Brandy's leotard. "No fire in a fireball performance! I told you their equipment wasn't to code. But do you ever listen?"

"Bryony, I take it?" I smiled and put a hand on my hip. "I hate to break up this tender reunion, but I have a schedule to keep."

Bryony's head jerked up as she noticed me for the first time. "Great. Please tell me I don't have to spend eternity with this moron."

I shrugged. Brandy hadn't actually made it onto the Posy Unit docket. It occurred to me, as the tent began to collapse, that maybe she *was* intended for the Lost Souls Unit.

"Time to move!" I put a hand on each of their backs and shoved them in the direction the center pole was falling, carefully avoiding its direct path.

A gaping hole formed at the tent's peak where a chunk of the canvas had burned away. The center pole pulled it along as we ran, and I tried to time its fall. I caught a glimpse of the smoke-filled sky through the hole and dug my fingers into the girls' shoulders just in time.

The tent collapsed around us, sending a cloud of soot and dirt into the air. When it settled, a dozen souls emerged from the charred bodies lying in a circle around the edges of the fallen canvas. Flaming debris dotted the ground, punctuating the black landscape. It reminded me a great deal of Hell. And then the screaming began.

CHAPTER TWO

*'None so deaf as those that will not hear.
None so blind as those that will not see.''
—Matthew Henry*

Purgatory Lounge was dead. A television buzzed in the corner where a pair of nephilim, the only other customers in the bar, sat watching the evening news with crinkled brows and heaping ashtrays.

Xaph's new waitress, a soul who worked days at the Three Fates Factory, delivered a pitcher and a frosted mug to my booth. Her strawberry-blond bangs fell forward, shadowing her face. She had trouble making eye contact, but that was common with most of the newer souls. Reapers made them nervous. My disheveled appearance probably didn't help.

Her hands shook as she took the heavy coin I offered. I wrapped my grimy fingers around the mug and nodded at the pitcher. "Go ahead and bring another if you see that reach half empty," I told her.

"Or half full," Gabriel said with a slight grin as he slid into the seat across from me. I tried to smile. His jokes were few and far between these days.

"I'll bring another mug," the waitress said, hurrying off.

"Make it two," Gabriel called after her. "Jenni is on her way," he said, answering my confused look. After a once-over, he added, "What happened to you?"

"Kevin played hooky again," I grumbled, wiping my hands down the legs of my jeans. It was no use. The crap wouldn't come off. I needed a shower, but I needed beer even more.

Gabriel pinched his lips together and cleared his throat. His wings twitched as he looked down and picked at the sleeve of his white robe, avoiding my annoyed stare.

"Come on. Let's hear it." I sighed and leaned back in the booth, crossing my arms.

Gabriel rolled his eyes. "He's your apprentice, Lana. You have to do something. If you don't straighten him out now, it's only going to get worse."

"You think I don't know that?" I leaned forward and put my elbows on the table before resting my forehead in my hands. "I've tried. Josie was so much better at this mentoring business. I don't know what I'm going to do with Kevin. He's never home, and on the rare occasions that he actually shows up for work, he's drunk."

Gabriel's eyes narrowed. "Drunk? How much time have you actually spent with Kevin since…?"

"You mean when I'm not working overtime to make up for his absence? Or when I'm not working odd assignments with Jenni to make ends meet?" I sighed. "Josie's…gone. Holly gave us a break on the rent, but her generosity has an expiration date. Kevin can't pay his share if he's not working.

Luckily, Jenni and I are workhorses and able to hold down the fort. For now.”

Gabriel frowned. “There’s a war raging outside. We’re all short on time—and patience. But that doesn’t mean we can afford to cut off those dear to us. You have to see to Kevin. He needs you right now.”

“Yeah? Well, I needed him today.” I slammed my fist on the table just as Jenni paused in front of our booth. She took one look at me and slid in next to Gabriel instead.

“Kevin bail again?” she asked, taking a fresh mug from our hesitant waitress. She poured herself and Gabriel each a glass. The waitress eyed the mostly empty pitcher and hurried off to fetch another.

Gabriel took a long drink and turned to Jenni. “Where did you say you spotted Kevin last week?”

Jenni gave me a cautious glance. “Leaving one of the apartments over on the west side, near the one we burned down last fall.”

“*Allegedly* burned down,” I snapped.

“Allegedly,” she echoed, no fight in her tone. The dark circles under her eyes and the slump in her shoulders zapped my desire to bitch about my awful day.

“I’ll try to have a heart-to-heart with Kevin the next time I see him. Whenever that is,” I said.

Jenni’s eyebrows shot up. “I don’t think a heart-to-heart is going to cut it, Lana. He needs *real* help.”

Like a switch, my anger returned. “And I’m not Josie. Yeah, I get it. What the hell do you suggest I do?”

Jenni opened her mouth, but Gabriel put a gentle hand on her arm.

"Lana, I think you should really consider taking him to Meng Po," he said.

My mouth fell open. "I know he's in pain, Gabriel. We all are. But wiping Josie from his memory is a little extreme, don't you think?"

"Damn it, Lana." Jenni shook her head. "You really are dense sometimes."

Gabriel reached across the table and took my hand before I could pull it away. "We're not suggesting that Meng erase Kevin's memory of Josie. We're suggesting that she erase his drug addiction."

I blinked stiffly, darting my eyes from Gabriel to Jenni.

Jenni's frustrated scowl softened, and she sighed. "Kevin is strung out on hellfire. Didn't you know?"

CHAPTER THREE

*"It takes considerable knowledge just to realize
the extent of your own ignorance."*
—Thomas Sowell

Kevin is strung out on hellfire. Didn't you know?

Jenni's words were a broken record inside my head as I sulked down the darkened streets of Limbo City, scuffing the soles of my boots along the pavement. Of course, I hadn't known about Kevin's addiction. Apparently, I was the *only* one who didn't. Even Jenni, Grim's second-in-command, who was every bit as busy as I, had noticed. I was the shittiest mentor ever.

The streetlights flickered on, and my insides tightened in false anticipation. I hadn't wandered the city at dusk much since last spring, when Tisiphone, a Greek fury, had tried to kill me. Streetlights turning on or off reminded me of her and triggered my anxiety. My mood darkened further, and by the time I made it back to Holly House, I was ready to maim anyone who looked at me wrong.

The lights under the bubbling fountain of holy water in the courtyard clicked on as I passed through the front gate, and my heart raced again. I snarled and swiped my hand through the spray arcing from a cherub's trumpet, feeling ridiculous that something so trivial had spooked me.

"Lana!"

I spun around, fists in the air. Warren, the nephilim in charge of arming the Nephilim Guard, Limbo City's primary defense, held up his hands in surrender. His pale wings shuddered nervously.

"Is this a bad time?" he asked.

"Yes, but I don't see that changing any time soon. What do you need?" I lowered my fists and tried not to look so rattled. I could feel my face protest as I forced the grimace out of my expression.

Warren carefully lowered his hands, and a smile lifted the corners of his mouth. "I have something special I've been working on for you. Would you care to take a look?"

I shrugged. "Sure, why not. I'll follow you up."

"Actually," he said, looking over his shoulder. "It's in my shop."

My interest piqued as I followed Warren around the side of the building to the small parking garage attached to Holly House. There were never more than a dozen vehicles tucked inside, so Holly had allowed Warren to set up a workshop in the back corner after he'd set off the fire alarm doing welding work in the spare room of his apartment.

Warren wasn't the average tenant at Holly House. In fact, other than him and my lot of misfit roommates, everyone else rooming at the holiest abode in Limbo City was either a deity or a high-ranked being associated with one of the subcommittees of the Afterlife Council.

Where my living situation was a team effort fueled by lucky—and hazardous—promotions, Warren's stay at Holly House was a result of a shifty business deal. With me. I had agreed to pay his first six months of rent in exchange for the double-headed battle axe I toted to work on not-so-casual Fridays.

Warren's new location drew the attention of more prestigious clients, like the Nephilim Guard. These days, he kept his licenses current, as well as his hygiene.

"You're gonna love it." Warren clapped his hands together and all but skipped through the parking garage. His giddiness for weapons and gadgets of war was disturbing yet well-deserved, considering his talent.

Warren used both hands to slide open a heavy, metal door. The shop lights flickered on, illuminating the shiny tools hanging from the back wall above his work table. A black tarp lay over something in the center of the room.

Warren circled it and grinned at me. "Ready?" he asked.

I nodded.

He pulled the tarp away with a magician's flair, revealing a sleek motorbike. The chrome wheels and exhaust pipes sparkled under the shop lights. Everything else was a soft, muted black, except for a shadowy skull painted on top of the gas tank. I walked closer so I could read the thin line of white script above it. *Graviora manent.*

"Greater dangers await," Warren said, translating the quote.

"I know. Demon defense requires a more advanced understanding of Latin." I smiled at his embarrassed expression and ran my hand over the bike's leather seat.

"Of course," Warren said. "You're teaching at the academy. I completely forgot."

"I wish I could." I sighed and gazed down the length of the bike. "This is amazing, Warren."

"You have no idea." He pointed down at the cap on the fuel tank. "It runs on holy water. You could literally fill it up at the fountain out front—but Holly probably wouldn't care for that," he quickly added. "There's a pump along the west wall of the garage. It's hooked into the plumbing system. I designed it myself." He beamed.

I fingered the dials on the handlebars. "I don't know much about motorcycles…"

Warren shook his wings out before tucking them in against his back. Then he nudged in closer to me and the bike. "It's not a traditional model. I've added so many enhancements, a previous knowledge probably wouldn't do you much good anyhow—"

"I don't even know how to ride a bicycle," I said.

Warren bit his lip and his brows cinched together. "Oh." He tilted his head from side to side. "Well, it's never too late to learn, right?"

I took a deep breath and gave him a pained look.

A smug grin spread across his face. "Trust me. This bike is totally worth it." He pointed at one of the dials. "It sprays holy water—and I programmed it to work in conjunction with coin travel." He fingered a round slot in the dash, just large enough to house a coin. "You can pre-enter your coordinates and get the hell outta Dodge with the press of a button. As long as you're not in a restricted area," he said. "The coin dial is also equipped with a backup system, so if the bike happens to break down, you can still transport it."

"Nice." I nodded. "Are you going to make these for the Nephilim Guard, too?"

"No. They can fly. Plus, they rarely leave the city, so the travel feature would be useless."

"Thanks, Warren. This was really nice of you."

He smiled sheepishly. "It's the least I could do. I know you're going through a lot, and I can't imagine Kevin is much help right now either—"

"Jesus, does everyone know?" I snapped.

Warren took a step back. "About Josie? There was a ceremony, Lana."

"Not that. Never mind." I blushed and cleared my throat. My mood swings were getting worse. I really needed to get a handle on them before I choked to death on my own foot.

I turned away from the bike and looked at Warren. "Seriously, thank you. I'll give it a go on one of my days off." *If I ever see one of those again.*

Warren gave me a parting nod, and I headed for the garage elevators. The bike was a sweet gesture, but it wasn't enough to distract my mind from the idea that my apprentice was a junkie. It was just one more thing on a growing list that I didn't know how to handle.

As the elevator neared the tenth floor, my stomach knotted. What if Kevin was in the condo? I didn't have the first clue how to go about talking to him. This was one of those situations I would have asked Josie for her advice on. Hell, it was one of those situations I probably would have dumped in her lap. No such luck this time.

The condo was dark when I entered, and I was ashamed by the rush of euphoric relief I felt. When I passed Kevin's room, a soft whimper crept out to greet me. I paused and clicked on the bedroom light.

My hellhound, Saul, lay across the unmade bed, his muzzle between his massive paws. He licked his nose and turned his sad eyes up to me. His sulking had grown worse after Coreen, my other hound, had given birth to a litter of puppies in Olympus. In exchange for one of the adorable abominations, Apollo and his oracle had agreed to keep Coreen until the pups were weaned. They weren't purebred. The puppies' father was undeniably one of Anubis's jackals.

I should have let Saul stay with his sister and her pups at the temple, but we were already short-handed at work. I had hoped leaving him in Kevin's care would soothe the kid, but I could at least appreciate the fact that he wasn't dragging my hound through his hellfire dens.

Kevin's room stank of sour clothes and beer. There was a layer of dust growing like mold on every surface, and cobwebs dotted the corners of the ceiling. It had been over a month since Josie's death, and if not for the untidy state of things, I could have easily pretended that she still lived here.

The closet door had been left open, and her pristine wardrobe hung next to the few casual outfits she'd helped Kevin pick out after his apprenticeship transferred to me. Her favorite book lay on top of her nightstand, a tasseled bookmark still tucked between the pages, and a half-empty glass of wine sat next to it as if maybe Josie had just gone to the restroom and would be back at any moment.

I swallowed the lump in my throat and softly patted my leg. Saul hopped off the bed and followed me down the hall. Kevin was doing hard drugs. Hellhound snuggles clearly weren't cutting it for him, and I needed comforting, too.

Farther down the hall, I noticed Jenni's cracked bedroom door. It was dark inside, a sign that she was working late. She couldn't sleep without a light, not since her week as a prisoner of the rebels. She didn't talk much about it, but I had walked in on one of her nightmares. Waking up in the dark, having to wonder if she was still in that hellhole… I couldn't even imagine.

I'd seen my share of horrors since the rebels began plaguing Eternity, and I had the scars to show for it. But, still, I considered myself lucky in a lot of ways. Besides, a pity party never did anyone any good.

And revenge was far sweeter.

CHAPTER FOUR

"Rank does not confer privilege or give power.
It imposes responsibility."
—Peter Drucker

At some ungodly hour in the morning, someone seized my shoulders and shook until I was sure I'd been turned into a dashboard bobblehead.

"*Lana,*" a course whisper begged. "Lana, please."

I peeled open my eyes to find Winston, the backstabbing former soul on the Throne of Eternity, hovering over me. His hair was a disaster, and his eyes were so wide that the whites seemed to glow in the dark.

The last time I'd seen Winston, I'd made it very clear that I never wanted to do so again. He had foreseen Josie's death and failed to warn me, and I didn't think I could ever forgive him for that.

"Lana," he rasped, digging his fingers into my arms.

I sat up and pushed away from him, bashing my head into the wall.

"What the hell are you doing here?" I said, rubbing the back of my throbbing skull. I glanced around the room, but we were alone. Saul had probably slunk back to Kevin's bed to mope some more.

Winston cringed and placed a finger over his mouth, trying to quiet my outburst. "I'm sorry," he whispered. "I need your help."

"I already told you, I'm done being your gopher. If you need something, go to Maalik." I rolled onto my side, giving Winston my back, and jerked the covers around me with a huff.

He circled the bed and knelt down, pushing his face close to mine. His frantic breath grazed my forehead. "Please, Lana. Naledi is missing."

"What?" I threw back the covers and shot upright.

"I think someone took her. The cottage looks like a tornado hit it. And I can't ask Maalik—he doesn't even know she exists, remember?"

I sat there for a moment in stunned silence.

As the throne soul, Naledi *literally* held the fate of Eternity in the palm of her hand. The Throne of Eternity was Grim's most fiercely guarded secret, one that he had held on to for over a millennium.

The soul who sat on the throne preserved the boundaries of the afterlives and contained the excess soul matter every year until it was distributed according to the Afterlife Council's ruling the night of the Oracle Ball. Of course, up until last year, no one but Grim had known that this was the throne soul's doing.

Everyone thought the power was Grim's alone to wield, and he was just benevolent enough to allow the deities of all faiths to have a say on the Afterlife Council. It was a convenient lie. I despised him for it, but I admired him for it, too.

While he had most definitely benefited undeservedly, he had relinquished just enough power to the others to keep the peace. Until now.

Grim's shortcoming had lain in him holding on to the secret for far too long. Khadija, the first soul who had sat on the throne, had been worked to exhaustion, to the point that her power slipped and created the needed opening for the rebels—those who craved war and the undue influence they thought they could obtain through force.

Khadija had tasked me with finding her successor. Grim's secrecy and hesitation left little time to complete the task, and it, unfortunately, drew the attention of the rebels. Winston had been the first usable soul I stumbled across, though he wasn't a true, original believer, which the throne required for a reign of any substantial length. After a few months, his power started to wane.

Grim was prepared to ignore the problem, desperate to keep the throne hidden. But the past life that made Winston's soul a candidate for the throne happened to be Egyptian, courtesy of Horus, the new Egyptian representative on the council. The sneaky old god blackmailed me into finding Winston's replacement. Though I hadn't expected Winston to jump the gun and trade places with the first soul I brought him.

I hated to admit it, but the fault was partially mine. I was supposed to slap a tracking bracelet on her wrist and go about business as usual. Instead, I'd brought her back to the throne realm to stay with Winston. *Stupid.*

That was how Naledi ended up on the throne, though no one knew that but dear Winston and me. He and Naledi had been playing a very dangerous game with Grim, hiding her whenever the boss man visited and convincing him that Winston was still in charge. It was a tightrope act, and they wouldn't be able to pull it off forever.

Amidst all the chaos, my one spot of relief had lain in the fact that I'd severed ties with the unruly Egyptian teens. When Grim found out about their guise, I didn't want to be anywhere near that shitstorm. Unfortunately, it looked like the weather had just taken a turn for the worse.

I glared at Winston. "You had one job. *One* job. How the hell could you lose her?"

Winston threw up his hands. "I was only gone for a minute. She needed something in the city."

"Shhhh. Let me think." I pressed a hand over my face and closed my eyes.

If the rebels had Naledi and knew her worth, it was hard telling what they were capable of. In the blink of an eye, Eternity could be transformed into an endless pit of fire. Every soul, whether in Heaven or Limbo or the sea, could be forsaken, left to their worst nightmares with no promise of redemption—no guarantee of returning to the mortal realm. It would be the end of everything. Armageddon.

I *so* did not want any part of this nightmare, but Winston was right. I was the only one who knew about Naledi, and I was pretty sure I was the only one who could locate her—well, besides Grim. But there was no coming back after a confession like that.

My head throbbed as I grasped for a different solution. Then it came to me—Horus's tracking bracelets. The original objective hadn't been to deceive Grim by switching the throne souls. It had been to find and tag a few new candidates so it would be easier to persuade Grim to let Winston go at the end of Horus's century-long term on the council.

"Lana," Winston whined, grabbing my arm again. "I'll do anything. Just please help me find Naledi. *Please*." He closed his eyes and folded his hands together, pushing them up under his chin as if he were praying to me.

"Okay," I hissed.

His eyes blinked open suddenly, and he threw his arms around my neck. "Thank you, thank you, thank you—"

"Get. Off," I said through gritted teeth. Winston jumped back, curling his hands into his chest as if he didn't know what else to do with them.

"Thank you, thank you," he said. I sliced my hand through the air, silencing him before he could start chanting his gratitude again.

"Just go home, Winston. I'll take care of this."

"Isn't there something I can do?" he asked.

"Yeah. Stay out of my way."

"But—"

"Do you want my help or not?" I folded my arms.

Winston nodded. "Okay, I'll go home. Thank you—"

"Don't start that again." I waved him off. "Just get out of here. I'll see what I can do."

Winston dug a large gray coin out of his pocket—one of the fancy ones that he'd bespelled to work even after coin travel had been deactivated in the city. He hesitated, fingering the token timidly, and then handed it to me. "You'll need this to get to the throne realm."

I took the coin with a grimace. It was the same one I'd all but told Winston to shove up his ass after Josie's death. He dug another out of his pocket and flipped it in the air, disappearing back to the throne realm before I could change my mind.

CHAPTER FIVE

"Our prime purpose in this life is to help others.
And if you can't help them, at least don't hurt them."
—Dalai Lama

I spent the rest of the morning digging through my closet, searching for the tracking bracelets. I'd hidden the silver compact that held them beneath the false bottom of a wooden tea crate stuffed with scarves and fancy shoes that I rarely had time to wear anymore.

The bracelets were old magic, and the unfamiliarity of it made me nervous. I spent half an hour digging through my old textbooks until I broke down and snuck into Kevin's room to scour Josie's shelves.

I found what I was looking for in the pages of a retired academy book titled *Understanding Soul Cycles*. I was sure that my mentor, Saul Avelo, had skipped over this particular subject. He wasn't fond of the Reaper Academy's lecture-style teaching and preferred to focus on field exercises.

After checking the index, I found half a page dedicated to the short-lived tracking bracelets. Their intent had been to allow mentors the ability to track a soul through the course of their apprentice's training, showing them first-hand the lifecycle of a human from the point where they reentered the mortal realm, right up to when their soul was harvested.

A single sentence detailed how the bracelets worked. It was vague, and I was ready to panic until I flipped the page and found a tiny diagram. The compact lid rotated and then folded in half, snapping together as if magnetic. It slid across the bottom half of the compact, locking in place once centered.

It looked like a sundial, especially when a shadow began dancing over its surface. It hummed and buzzed before the shadow finally spread out to cover the entire disc. A set of coordinates blinked through the darkness, disappearing after a moment like a thermometer's reading.

I'd failed to scribble down the numbers, but it didn't matter. I recognized the location. I'd been there too many times to count. Tartarus. My heart crawled up my throat, and I had to remind myself to breathe.

The alarm on my bedside table went off. I groaned, recalling my other responsibilities. It was Monday. Not only did I have a boatload of souls to harvest but I also had the demon defense course at the academy later that evening. On the plus side, if tracking down Naledi got me killed, I wouldn't have to worry about teaching anymore.

CHAPTER SIX

*"Perseverance is the hard work you do
after you get tired of doing the hard work you already did."*
—*Newt Gingrich*

"This sucks." Kate Evans sighed as she looked over the docket I'd just handed her. Alex Grayson, her girlfriend and fellow Posy, held out her list to compare.

"I know." I cringed and moved on down the deck of my ship. "No one's docket looks pretty today. Trust me."

Tyler Ives rolled his eyes. "You know what would make them look better? If your apprentice had one of these, too."

He waved his docket in my face, pulling it back when I narrowed my gaze on him. His lips pressed together in a frustrated line, and his scalp turned pink, visible beneath his buzzed hair.

The military look was typical for a lot of the younger male reapers. I suppose they thought it made them look older or more serious. I didn't care for it, and I was glad Kevin hadn't chopped his boyish curls.

Tyler was having a hard time remembering his place. Not only was he a generation younger than I was and under my captainship but he was also one of the greenest members on the unit. Just before her death, Josie had chosen him and

Molly Driver to join us. I wasn't overly fond of Tyler, but I couldn't bring myself to question Josie's judgment. Not now. Besides, I was still pretty happy with her other choice.

Molly gave me a tight smile as I handed over her docket. "I'm ambitious, sweetie, but they're right. Harvesting has been rough these past few weeks." Her thin brows arched over her giant, green eyes. I wanted to be angry, but I could tell she was sincere.

Arden, of course, didn't say anything. There were circles under his eyes, the same as the rest of us, but it took a lot for the African Posy to complain.

"The week before the Oracle Ball is always the worst. Next week will be better. I promise," I said.

Everyone sighed and grumbled a bit, but they eventually made their way down to the harbor dock so they could coin off to their harvests. I felt guilty for doctoring my list, but I had to do something if I was expected to squeeze in saving Eternity before teaching class.

I hadn't skipped out on my unit altogether. I'd cherry-picked four small lots of sea-bound souls from the master Posy docket. Molly was right. The heavy harvesting was running us all ragged, and there was no way I could completely unburden myself for the entire day without forcing them to work all night. I wasn't *that* big of a jerk.

I hated dumping souls in the Sea of Eternity. Half of the atheists and agnostics who ended up there were no worse than the souls frolicking through Heaven's gates, and the other half was no better than the lot roasting in Hell. It wasn't fair from any angle, but it was part of the job. At least not having to make deliveries to the afterlives shaved off a couple of hours from my day. I didn't know if it would be enough, but I had to try.

By midafternoon, I'd made it back to the condo to change, check on Saul, and grab my axe. It was clunky and uncomfortable under my robe, but I didn't want to look too suspicious as I entered the travel booth across the street from Holly House.

I didn't input the exact coordinates that the tracking compact had suggested, not wanting to find myself in the middle of a hoard of rebels. Instead, I put in a set I was equally familiar with that would give me a good vantage point.

When I emerged in Tartarus, I ducked down atop a mountain ledge that bordered the ruins of Beelzebub's summer manor. The tracking bracelet's coordinates pinpointed Naledi near where the gardens had once curled around the backside of the property and stretched out toward the mountains.

I peered over the long expanse of wasteland, searching the rubble for any sign of the soul or her captors, and tried not to think about what had been. The happiest days of my life had been spent here, and the ache in my chest was an annoying distraction that I couldn't afford right now.

A flicker of illumination caught my eye, and my attention zeroed in on a crumbling stone wall that had once bordered the garden. I squinted, and the light came again, shimmery and blue, peeking around the edges of the wall. My pulse trembled hopefully. Maybe I would be lucky for a change.

I had to get closer to find out.

The heat was unbearable, and with my axe in tow, descending to the desert floor was grueling. Several windstorms had blown through over the past few weeks, and the debris from the manor's destruction had set the foundation for a series of low-rising dunes. I maneuvered around them, trying to stay out of view while keeping my eye on the blue light.

The wind pushed gently, stirring the sand around my ankles. It carried the subtle stench of soot and rot. Barely a month ago, the ripeness of the garden would have reached out to greet me here, with sweet notes of forbidden fruit.

The sky was beginning to melt into an orangey-pink hue, a sign of the approaching night. It reflected off the River Styx, making the waters appear as if they were bleeding into the dark red sand along the beach. The blue light sparkled in contrast, spilling out around the edges of the bit of wall.

When I finally reached it, I took another look around, confirming that no rebels were lying in wait. A muffled sound finally urged me to venture past the wall, my axe held at the ready.

"What the—?" I looked around again, certain that a hoard of demons was just waiting to jump me.

The soul, while clearly an original believer, was not Naledi. Not by a long shot. It—or *he*, rather—sat with his back to the crumbling stone, his feet and hands bound together, and strips of cloth tied around his eyes and mouth.

I retrieved the tracking compact from my pocket and tried to activate it, but despite following the steps precisely as I had that morning, nothing happened. I resisted the urge to throw the damn thing on the ground and stomp it into a zillion pieces, and instead, shoved it back into my pocket.

I knelt down in front of the soul and yanked the blindfold and gag away first. He took a deep, shuddering breath and then screamed. It pierced through my ear like an icepick, and my hand involuntarily reached out and smacked him.

"*Jeeesus*. What's wrong with you?" I pressed a hand to the side of my head as I glared at him.

The soul's cheeks puffed out with indignant rage. With his frumpy, white robe and bald head, he looked like a melty ice cream sundae with a cherry on top.

"I do *not* belong here. I was devout. Do you know what that means, you heathen?" he barked at me.

"Heathen?" I arched an eyebrow and moved to put the gag back over his mouth.

"Wait! Wait. I-I can prove it. Really." He nodded vigorously.

"I don't need your proof. I just need to know how you got here," I said, holding up the gag menacingly.

"It must have been a demon. That's the only way, isn't it? I certainly don't belong here. I would have been a saint in another time, you know—"

"Was there another soul here with you?" I asked, looking around for any sign of Naledi. I'd take any original believer I could get my hands on, what with the pickle we were in, but this guy looked like he had the potential to be an even bigger pain in the ass than Winston.

"What?" The new soul snorted as if I'd insulted him. "No. What good would another soul do a demon if he already had me?"

"Save it for Peter." I dug out the coin Winston had given me and flipped it, taking us both out of the wreckage of my love life and into the throne realm.

CHAPTER SEVEN

*"You will not be punished for your anger,
you will be punished by your anger."*
—Buddha

Winston sat on the front porch of the cottage. He rocked back and forth, grasping his knees tightly as he stared off into nothingness. When he caught sight of me across the lawn, he jumped up and tripped over his own feet in a rush to greet us.

"Who's this? Where's Naledi?" he stammered, gesturing wildly with both hands.

"I have no idea," I said, pushing past him up to the cottage's front door. I waited until we were all safely inside before continuing. "This is the only soul I found near where the bracelet coordinates sent me."

"That's impossible. I don't even see a bracelet on him. You must have gone to the wrong location. Try again," he demanded. His voice echoed in the cavernous room.

Winston and Naledi hadn't been at the cottage for very long, but neither of them seemed overly interested in decorating the place as far as I could tell. A single, hanging incense burner graced the corner of the foyer. The empty stone walls stretched upward and rolled into a domed ceiling that featured a wide, circular skylight. Daylight spilled down on us, illuminating the swirls of dust left in Winston's wake as he paced.

The new soul curled his nose before turning to thrust his bound hands at me. "Do you mind? This is no way to treat a priest."

I rolled my eyes and fingered the rope knots as I addressed Winston. "I went to the right location, but Naledi must have been moved. I don't know why they left saint grouchy pants here behind, but he *is* an original believer, for what it's worth."

"I don't give a shit what he is. Try again!" Winston shouted, stamping his foot.

I paused and glared at him over my shoulder.

"Please," he added as if an afterthought, and folded his hands together, squeezing until his knuckles popped.

I turned back to the new soul and crooked a finger under his ropes again. "I can't. The tracking device isn't working right. I need to go back to Holly House and take another look at Josie's bookshelf. I'm sure she had a text with more information on how this thing works."

Winston tilted his head back and growled his frustrations. Then he pointed at the priest. "Well, what am I supposed to do with him? Shouldn't you be dumping him in the sea or something?"

I shrugged. "I thought he could stay here with you for now." They both scoffed as if I'd suggested they start a knitting club. "He's an original believer. You're an original believer—sort of. Besides, if worse comes to worst, we may need him."

Winston's eyes bulged in horror. "Don't be stupid. I can't put him on the throne. We need Naledi back, immediately."

I finished freeing the priest and faced Winston as I placed both hands on my hips. "Okay. Your tone…it's not working for me right now."

Winston pinched his lips together, and his face scrunched up, turning red and gnarled until he finally exploded with rage. "You'll find Naledi, or I'll tell Grim everything!"

I stepped forward, poking my finger into his chest. "Go ahead!" I shouted back. "I wonder what he'll do with you once he finds out how worthless you are. Either way, you'll be out of my hair."

Winston screeched, turning in a wide circle with his hands on his head. He finally stopped when he bumped the hanging incense holder in the corner. Ash drifted from its open edge onto the floor as Winston gripped it with one hand and yanked it from its chain. He snarled at me and threw the rest of the burner's contents in my face.

"You little shit!" I gagged on the pungent ash and wiped the back of my hand across my mouth. Then I found my coin.

Winston took a step toward me. "Wait! I'm sorry," he said, his hands outstretched.

But I'd already tossed the coin into the air. As it fell into my open palm, I flipped Winston off with my free hand until the foyer disappeared.

CHAPTER EIGHT

"Nothing makes us so lonely as our secrets."
—Paul Tournier

I stepped out of the travel booth across from Reapers Inc. still coughing and covered in ash. My heart drummed murderously, and the sour taste of bile stung the back of my throat as my vision blurred. I bent over and shook my head like a dog. Giant gray flakes dotted the sidewalk.

"Rotten, ungrateful bastard," I grumbled to myself as I fingered my curls and slapped at my robe.

When I finished my little grooming dance, I looked up to find Maalik gawking at me from the curb.

"Do I even want to know?" he asked with a lopsided grin.

His silver-tinted wings were folded against his shoulder blades and trailed down the length of his black robe. I couldn't help but envision them in a more sensual setting. A twinge in my chest gave me pause, but I quickly brushed it away. I still had a soft spot for the broody angel, but our moment had passed. Our differences were such that we only seemed to come together over our mutual desire to crush the rebels.

I sighed and shook my head. "Long day."

It was best to leave it at that for Maalik. He knew about Winston, but I was pretty sure he didn't go to the throne realm often, and he definitely didn't approve of me visiting.

Maalik put his hands into the pockets of his robe and tilted his head up at the Reapers Inc. building. "Heading in?"

"Yeah. Fancy job titles come with fancy paperwork." I gave him a pained smile that he returned. He knew all about the fancy paperwork as a member of the Afterlife Council.

"I'll ride up with you," he said, turning to open the front door for me.

The lobby of Reapers Inc. sparkled. The soaring windows were spotless, and the floors had been polished until they reflected the natural light with a celestial intensity. Silver and gold tinsel garlands hung from the ceiling, and giant glass vases stuffed with white tulips sat in every corner.

I followed Maalik to the elevators, and we waited for a group of Nephilim Guard trainees to exit a car before we stepped inside. A massive poster advertising the upcoming Oracle Ball stretched across the back wall of the elevator. The doors slid closed behind us and, suddenly, we were alone in the tight space. Our eyes met for a brief second and then averted.

Maalik cleared his throat. "Are you, uh, going to the…?"

"The ball?" I asked, glancing over my shoulder at the poster. "No. I don't think so."

Maalik's brows lifted gently. "Why not? You haven't had a day off in weeks. It might do you some good to relax a bit."

I leaned away from him. "And why exactly do you know my work schedule?"

He blushed. "I'm on the council. Knowing everything is part of the job description."

"I'm sure you're just as informed about every reaper, right?" Heat crawled up my neck and spread across my cheeks.

Maalik blew out a deep breath, and then his soft expression grew darker as he inhaled again. He reached out and pinched a flake of ash off the sleeve of my robe.

"Harvest a fire today?" he asked with a frown as he rubbed his fingers together.

"I don't know. You tell me," I said hotly, just as the elevator pinged, and the doors opened to the seventy-third floor—the Afterlife Council headquarters.

Maalik's mouth hung open as if he had more to say, but Cindy Morningstar, the council representative for the Abrahamic Hells—and the person responsible for Beelzebub's undercover operation—waited in the hallway.

Her smile was placid, but the twinkle in her eyes betrayed her provocative nature. "Councilor." She nodded to Maalik before turning to me. "Captain Harvey."

I ground my teeth together and forced myself to nod back at her. "Good evening."

I hadn't seen Cindy since everything went south with Bub. She didn't know he had revealed their secrets to me, and I was pretty sure she would roast both him and me over a fire like a couple of marshmallows if she found out.

Cindy reached out and lightly brushed her fingers across my arm. "I am so sorry about what happened with Beelzebub. I don't blame you at all for trashing his flat in Pandemonium.

I probably would have burned the entire building to the ground." Her demon eyes searched mine, and I felt a trickle of sweat trail down the back of one ear.

"Thanks," I said weakly, my breath trapped in my chest like an overinflated balloon.

The elevator doors began to close, and Maalik shot out a hand to stop them as if he had completely forgotten that this was his stop. He gave me a forced smile as he stepped into the hall with Cindy.

"Good to see you again, Lana," Maalik said.

"You, too." I swallowed and gave them both a parting nod as the doors closed, and the elevator continued up to the seventy-fifth floor, where my office was located.

Ellen glanced up from her desk when I emerged. Her nose crinkled as she took in my dusty hair and robe. "Oh, honey. I do not envy you on days like this," she said. Then she jumped up and pointed at the glossy floor. "You should probably take off your robe there. The cleaning crew just left, and Grim would flip if you tracked"—she waved her hand at me—"whatever that is through the office."

I groaned and dug out my clipboard before pulling the robe off, creating a halo of dust around my head. Ellen cringed as if deciding she had made the wrong call.

I wadded up the robe and set it on her desk, giving her my saddest puppy-dog eyes. "Tell me you've got the good stuff on hand."

Ellen puckered her lips as she shuffled through her top desk drawer, coming away with a handful of foil-wrapped truffles.

"You're the best." I snatched up the chocolates and blew her a kiss as I headed down the hall to my office.

The light on my phone blinked at me as I opened the door. The pulsing red reflected off my desk, and my stomach tightened as I realized that the cleaning crew had been through here, as well. All of my files were stacked in a neat pile. The wastebasket was empty, and someone had watered the potted Peace Lily that my old classmate, Mira Hart, had sent with her condolences after Josie's death.

I'd left the plant in my office hoping it would appease Grim until I had time to hire a decorator. Ellen had set up several appointments for me, but I'd missed them all due to my insane workload.

I tossed my clipboard onto my desk and pressed play on the phone.

"Lana, it's Ross. I know you're keeping busy hours these days, but I really need to speak with you when you have a moment. I'd rather not address this formally."

Ross was the captain of the Nephilim Guard. He was also Gabriel's roommate. It seemed strange to me that he was calling, and while his voice was tense, it didn't sound like he was in immediate need of my assistance. He would have to wait. I had exactly thirty minutes to scribble out a summary of the day and fill in my report card. Then it was off to the academy to teach bright, young reapers how to slay demons.

CHAPTER NINE

*"Education is a better safeguard of
liberty than a standing army."*
—Edward Everett

Attendance at the academy's demon defense course was lighter since Bub's departure. Twenty percent of the students had dropped the class after the Lord of the Flies was outed as a traitor. Another twenty percent left after I was named the new professor. Kevin had ditched too, but that had more to do with his grief than any suspected incompetence on my part. At least, I hoped so.

The few reapers who remained were too young to hold my meager experience against me—or just plain petrified by the sudden influx of demonic rebel activity. Limbo City's coin travel restrictions were little comfort, considering the alarming number of lairs the Nephilim Guard had uncovered in the past month.

Limbo was no longer the neutral city beyond the veil, and quite a few businesses had suffered from the declining tourism, too. Several had packed up shop and headed back to their motherlands over the Sea of Eternity, including the owner of my favorite Thai restaurant and the Muses Union House.

A few of the abandoned buildings had been vandalized and marked with the sign of the rebels, a backward E in dripping, red spray paint. The media had a new expert interpret the symbol every week. Sometimes, it was a threat that Eternity would regress back to a simpler, more barbaric time. Sometimes, it stood for existential quantification, a taunting reminder that the rebels still walked among us. I liked to pretend that it was backward by accident, scrawled by a bunch of illiterate shmucks who didn't know any better. It would have been easier to think so if Bub weren't one of them.

The few businesses that were hanging on in Limbo had taken some more extreme safety measures. Athena put two of her enchanted mannequins out front to guard her boutique and the neighboring stores. They marched back and forth down the sidewalk in last season's castoffs—with the sale tags in plain sight, of course—toting spears donated by Artemis.

Xaphen, the fire demon who owned Purgatory Lounge, had upped his security, too—though he was more worried about the good guys sabotaging his bar. Unbeknownst to him, a group of illegal demons had been meeting up at Purgatory last spring. A Nephilim Guard raid had caught the culprits, but the scene had pushed Xaph's reputation into murky, gray territory. No one wanted to be caught rubbing elbows with a rebel. It was a wonder he could still pay his bills.

The city hadn't completely shriveled up and died, though. Besides my class, the academy was actually thriving. Most classrooms were filled to capacity, and attendance and test scores were at an all-time high.

Young and old reapers alike were haunted by the realization that we were most definitely not immortal beings, and they jumped on every opportunity to improve their chances of survival through the war. Without a devoted following on the mortal side, the soul matter coursing through my kind was a more fragile variety. We were as organic on this side of the grave as humans were on the mortal side—except we didn't age. How's that for a job perk? Forget the dental plan.

It wasn't unjust paranoia motivating the reapers. More and more demon attacks were being reported on the job. There was no distinguishable pattern. It was random chaos. While the Demon Suffrage Movement in the city had reduced attacks on innocent demons, the recovery rooms at Meng Po's temple had been refilled with injured reapers, and a disturbing number of souls were being reported as CNH.

After my psychotic outburst over Bub's bogus betrayal, in which I'd destroyed a priceless sculpture at his flat and launched a nasty assault on the skank of a succubus he was *pretending* to court, I'd been left alone by the rebels. I guess they thought if I was ballsy enough to come after the Lord of the Flies, then I probably wasn't an easy mark or someone to be trifled with. Redefining "crazy ex-girlfriend" had its perks.

By the time I pushed through the academy doors Monday night, the first bell had already rung. The halls were crammed with reapers, but also a handful of the nephilim. The Guard was really growing now that Grim had granted the recruits permanent residency in Limbo City. They had rented out a few classrooms at the academy for their training program.

Grace Adaline, my former professor, who had guilted me into taking over Bub's class, spotted me from across the hall and dipped her head to give me a patronizing look over the top of her glasses. She tapped the watch on her wrist as the students began to filter into the classrooms. I played stupid and tossed her a carefree wave as I ducked inside my room, just as the final bell rang.

Jack, Bub's demonic ex-butler, waited for me at the door. He held out his hands for the mountain of books I carried and followed me to my desk, humming a cheerful tune.

"What are you so happy about?" I asked, trying not to sound like a jealous curmudgeon.

He straightened his jacket, and I noticed the shiny green bowtie under his chin. "I have a date to the Oracle Ball," he said, his horns held high, and a smile splitting his wrinkly face in half like a giant walnut.

"That's nice." I felt my teeth clench as I tried out a smile. The expression was difficult to manage lately. "Who's the lucky girl?"

"Lady Meng," he chirped.

I recoiled and gave him a wide-eyed glare.

"I know! Isn't it fantastic?" he said, misreading my expression entirely.

Jack worked part-time at Meng's temple in exchange for room and board. He'd been beaten and left homeless after Bub's summer manor was torched, so when Maalik and I brought him to Meng's to be patched up, he'd practically imprinted on the old gal like a baby duckling. An old, demonic baby duckling in an eighteenth-century tailcoat.

I wondered if Meng had whipped up a special Viagra tea for the night of the Oracle Ball, and then I shook my head, refusing to let my mind wander into creepier territory.

"Midterms," I snapped. "Midterms are two weeks out." I waved my hand at the small herd of reapers clustered in the front few rows of desks.

Their shoulders cinched in, and their eyes swelled in horror. A few of them glanced nervously at the charred spot along the back row where I had incinerated the desk of a smart-mouthed brat before sending her packing at the beginning of the school year. That's when they all started addressing me formally and with downturned eyes.

"Yes, yes. Very important turning point for these growing minds," Jack said.

He turned and shuffled through the folders on my desk until he found the one containing the study guides he'd worked up. Most of the questions were multiple choice Latin incantations. Even though I was well-trained, Jack's Latin was still far better than mine. I was lucky to have him in the classroom, especially considering my demanding day job. After midterms, I planned to take the class out for field exercises, where I hoped to better prove my worth as an instructor.

A knock came from the classroom door, and I grimaced, worried it might be Grace, come to give me a lecture on punctuality. I turned to Jack with an exasperated pout.

"I'll pass these out," he said, hurrying off with the stack of study guides before I could protest. I dragged myself over to the door and peeked out into the hallway.

Ross greeted me with a long face. "I'm really sorry, Lana, but this couldn't wait any longer," he said, holding out his hand to the side in a silent request for me to join him.

I closed the classroom door behind me and walked farther down the hall, motioning for him to follow me out of my students' earshot. When I stopped and faced Ross, he removed his crested helmet and ran a hand through his silver curls. His forehead crinkled, and his brows dipped sullenly.

"What's the matter?" I asked, placing a hand on his arm.

"I hate to be the bearer of bad news," he whispered. His wings fluttered anxiously, making a soft whistling noise as they brushed the shoulder pieces of his armor.

"Sometimes, it can't be avoided," I said, trying to sound more encouraging than I felt.

Ross pressed his hand over the top of mine and looked me in the eyes. "We arrested a drug lord in the harbor this afternoon."

My breath caught, and I resisted the urge to pull my hand back. I had a sinking feeling that I knew where the conversation was headed.

Ross licked the corner of his mouth and swallowed. "He was seen near your ship, shortly after Kevin arrived at the harbor."

I nodded and blinked stiffly, trying to clear the red from my vision. "I understand. I'll take care of it."

Kevin wasn't just frequenting the hellfire dens on the west side of town. He was having the shit delivered to my boat. Gabriel was right. He needed help. A boot in the ass seemed like a good start to me.

Ross let go of my hand and took a slow step back, regarding me with cautious, pitying eyes. "Protocol would have been to search your ship and take him in, but I know what you've all been through—"

"I said I'll take care of it." I pressed my lips together, trying to keep myself from saying anything more that I might regret. Ross was doing me a favor, but my gratitude was buried beneath a thick layer of helpless guilt and fury. I'd have to thank him properly some other time.

"Goodnight, Captain Harvey," he said, giving me a short bow before putting his helmet back on and disappearing down the hall.

I waited outside the classroom for a few moments, trying to rein in my wrath, but it was no use. Class would be letting out early tonight. My top student had fallen behind, and that was unacceptable.

︿︿

CHAPTER TEN

"Every form of addiction is bad, no matter
whether the narcotic be alcohol or morphine or idealism."
—Carl Jung

The entire class seemed grateful for the early release, especially after Jack had passed out the study guides. They crinkled the pages in their sweaty hands and shuffled out of the classroom, faces pressed into textbooks like the end was nigh. I hated to think that they might be right.

As we dispersed across campus, there was only one cheerful face in our gloomy little crowd. Jack practically skipped beside me.

"I'm going to stop and pick up some flowers on the way home. Do you think Meng would like that?" he asked, folding his gloved hands together in front of him.

I shrugged. "It's hard telling with Meng, but I definitely wouldn't buy her tea. Ever."

"Oh dear, no. That goes without saying, does it not?" He pressed a hand to my shoulder as we reached the travel booth on the corner. "Take care, Lana."

"You, too," I said with a quick nod.

Jack headed farther down Council Street toward Ghost Alley. Flora's flower shop was a block south, and it was only another two blocks back to Meng's from there. Even though the rebels were more interested in their graffiti as of late, I still worried about Jack's safety.

The rest of the academy night classes hadn't let out yet, so I didn't have to wait long at the travel booth, which was good since I had the creepy-crawly sensation that someone was watching me. I'd been ambushed enough times that it was a wonder I hadn't grown a pair of eyeballs in the back of my skull.

When it was my turn to step into the booth, I paused and took a quick glance around. The sky had darkened to a dusty gray, and the fading light glazed the rooftops of the city before dissolving into shadow at street level.

The small patch of woods that sat behind the academy was darker still, the tops of the evergreens silhouetted into spears aimed at the sky. In the shadows they left across the academy lawn, I sensed movement. A shiver rocked my shoulders as I quickly dropped a coin into the travel booth's slot.

My hyper-paranoia didn't diminish until I was safely inside the condo. I dropped my books on the dining table and fed Saul a scoop of Cerberus Chow. I was exhausted, and it would have been nice to just call it a night, but Ross's warning was a constant nag in the back of my mind.

As I left Holly House, the feeling of unease returned. I patted my pocket, making sure I had remembered my angelica mace before heading toward the booth across the street. The travel restrictions in Limbo City were meant to keep the rebels out, but seeing how futile that was, the booths seemed like a

huge inconvenience—unless you were trying to spy on someone.

Night had fully fallen by the time I arrived at the harbor.
A damp fog wove its way through the boats and ships. I
yawned and blinked a few times as my eyes adjusted to the
harsh new bulbs that had been installed in the dock lanterns.
The unnatural brightness lit up the marina like a concert stage.
It was intended to up security, but I felt entirely too exposed
not being able to see the horizon past the halo of blinding
light.

I hugged myself and shuddered, wishing I had remembered to grab a jacket while I was at the condo. Then I glanced
back at the two nephilim who were standing watch at the entrance to the harbor, wondering if I might catch a glimpse of
my tail. The feeling that I was being watched had returned the
moment I left Holly House.

The streetlights dotting the market area revealed empty
sidewalks as far as I could see in either direction. One of the
guards turned to follow my gaze. He looked back at me with
a curious frown that I couldn't quite decipher. Either he
thought he had missed something, or he was trying to decide
if I was nuts. I gave him a friendly, two-fingered salute and
headed down the main pier toward my ship.

This late in the evening, the dock was devoid of reapers.
The day's harvests had been delivered to their afterlives, and
as overtaxed as everyone was lately, I was sure most reapers
were either in bed or drinking away their troubles in one of
the few dive bars around town that didn't hold a candle to
Purgatory.

As I neared my ship, soft music trickled from an open cabin window. Seawater slapped at the hull, rocking the boat gently in time with the song. The dock lanterns were so bright that they reflected off every surface, and I couldn't tell if a light was on anywhere inside.

I crept up the ramp and slipped back to my cabin to find a flashlight. Then I followed the music up to the forecastle cabin, the one Kevin had been remodeling for himself and Josie. The rancid smell of burnt sulfur filtered through the door, turning my stomach.

The hellfire that Kevin was at the mercy of was different from the kind Maalik could summon to smite his enemies. It was more of a slang name for the drug, but its origins were similarly rooted in the Abrahamic hell region. Thorns from the fruit of the Zaqqum tree, found only in the flaming bowels of Jahannam, were burned to ash, diluted with holy water, and then injected. It was the main reason the two substances required a license to carry in Limbo City—though drug dealers weren't exactly known for their legitimate transactions.

I wrapped my hand around the doorknob to Kevin's cabin and found it unlocked. It was as if he wanted to be caught. I pushed open the door. The room was dark. Heavy curtains hung over the windows, blocking out the dock lanterns. A greenish ember glowed in an ashtray on a bedside table, the meager light outlining Kevin's still form, face-down on the bed.

I dropped the flashlight and used both hands to roll him onto his back. "Kevin? Wake up," I said, slapping at his face and chest.

He groaned as his eyes cracked open and he glared up at me. "What do you want?"

I slumped on the bed and blew out a long breath, running my hands over my face and through my hair as my heart reeled from the sudden jolt of panic. "*Christ*, I thought you were dead."

"I wish," he slurred.

This close, I could see the yellow tint to his eyes. His lips were dry and cracked, and his breath was labored as if he had been fighting demons all day rather than lying in bed, high as a hellcat.

His eyes started to close again, but I shook his arm. "Get up. You're coming home with me." I stood and pulled back a curtain, letting the dock lights blast into the room like a spotlight.

"Whatever." Kevin turned away from the light and reached for the smoldering ashtray, but I was faster. I snatched up the dish and tossed it out the open window, right into the sea. The flood of light had also revealed an open syringe case, and I sent it out right behind the ashtray.

Kevin's eyes opened fully then. "You have no right—"

"I have every right." I picked up my flashlight and pointed it in his face. "You're doing illegal drugs on *my* ship."

Kevin squinted and raised his arm to shield his eyes. "I'm not hurting anyone. Leave me alone."

"The Nephilim Guard arrested your dealer on the dock tonight, and they would have hauled your ass off too if Ross hadn't stepped in. You got lucky, but it won't happen again."

I spotted his robe in the corner and bent to pick it up. A lighter fell out of the pocket, and Kevin rolled off the bed, reaching for it. I stomped on the lighter, cracking the cheap plastic and splattering fluid across the floorboards.

"Seriously?" Kevin glared up at me. I tossed his robe in his face.

"Get up. We're going home," I said again, pushing more venom into my tone.

"Fine," Kevin snapped. He stood and pulled the robe over his head with a huff. Then he swung his hand at the door. "After you, *boss lady*," he said, spitting each syllable.

I tried to swallow my anger and turned to walk out of the cabin. I hadn't made it two steps across the deck before the door slammed shut behind me. The lock clicked as I turned around.

"Dammit, Kevin!" I slammed my fist on the door.

"Go away," he shouted from the other side. "Don't you have someone else's life to ruin?"

"Kevin." My voice was a hoarse whisper. Tears came, but I blinked them away. "Kevin," I said again, louder. "This isn't what Josie would have wanted for you."

There was a bitter, muffled laugh, followed by a sob. I jumped back when something hit the door from the other side.

Kevin growled. "How would you know what she wanted? You were too busy fucking a traitor."

"That's not fair, Kevin." I slammed my palm against the door. Tears pushed behind my eyes again, but a vibration in my pocket stole my attention.

The tracking compact buzzed in my hand as I retrieved it. It had never done that before, not without me prompting it. I slid the magnetic top into place and waited for the coordinates to surface. I committed them to memory and then shoved the compact back into my pocket, glancing around the deck nervously as I did.

"Kevin," I shouted through the door. "We're not done here. We'll talk more tomorrow when you're sober."

"Fuck off," he said so softly that the door almost muffled his words entirely.

"Right." *That went well.*

I sighed and walked down the ramp to the dock. There was no sense trying to talk to Kevin while he was high. I felt useless.

The weight of the tracking disc pressed into my thigh, and a responsibility greater than my apprentice pushed to the front of my mind. I could just barely see the two nephilim guards in the distance. They weren't looking my way, so I quickly pulled out a coin and rolled it in my hand as I whispered the new coordinates.

CHAPTER ELEVEN

"Come away, O human child!
To the waters and the wild
With a fairy, hand in hand,
For the world's more full of weeping than you can understand."
—William Butler Yeats

Night hadn't quite gripped Summerland yet. It was a vast realm, despite its modest voice on the council, and the coordinates I'd used spit me out in an unfamiliar span of wilderness.

The heat of the day had tapered off to a comfortable coolness in the absence of the sun, and the sky melted down the horizon like the sticky residue of a banana split. I hiked up a rocky hill and looked all around, taking in the whole of the land while I still could in the fading light.

About fifty yards behind me, a field of tall grain swayed in the wind. A unicorn grazing under a lone frankincense tree lifted its head to observe me. It let out a startled snort, provoking a flock of phoenixes to abandon their roosts in the tree.

To the north and south, lush evergreens bordered the hilly countryside, their branches overlapping and weaving together in a daunting barricade. There was no trail to be found.

Opposite the field, an endless sea stretched out to meet the horizon, as still and smooth as glass. It reflected the small smear of bright sky and the stars piercing the settling darkness. For a moment, it looked as if the world had opened its mouth to me. I felt I could leap from the rocky hill and plunge down the gullet of the universe.

The ground beneath my feet began to tremble, and the water rippled, breaking the illusion. I crouched low and held on to the hill with both hands, cursing myself for falling into what was clearly a trap.

The sea began to bubble, and a small island broke the surface. Sandy beaches circled a cluster of trees, and as the sky darkened, flickering lights came into focus, dotting the shore. The whisper of bells and drums carried across the water. The sound, beautiful and conflicted, tickled my ears. I couldn't decide if it was an invitation or a threat.

My breath caught as I realized where the coordinates had taken me. This was the forbidden border of Summerland where it touched the realm of the faeries before bleeding into the mortal realm. I'd seen the field before, from the opposite side that bordered the more neutral faerie glades where mingling with the fair folk was safest. The Sea of Avalon marked the end of Summerland proper, and the island rising up in the distance was no doubt one of the sacred isles of the fey.

Some of the faeries could cross over from this side of the veil to the other. And some of the older pagan deities were linked very strongly with the fey, which is why their territory could only be reached through Summerland from the afterlife. The path was open to very few others. The fey were a fickle bunch, and while they honored their treaties, they knew all the loopholes when it came to playing with outsiders in their own territory. They were not the bread-breaking sort, as made evident by their inability to conform to either side of the grave.

A heavy mist rose up to swallow the tail-end of the sunset as the sea calmed again until I could only see a faint outline of the island and its dreamy lights, flickering out at me like a secret code. Through the mist, I noticed a small boat cutting through the water like a shark. I backed down the hill and pressed myself against its damp roughness. It was the only hiding place available unless I wanted to risk getting impaled by Mr. Pointy back in the field.

I'd never had problems with any of the fair folk, and I intended to keep it that way. *Unless they're consorting with the rebels.* I swallowed and pulled myself in tighter against the hill.

It was true that we'd encountered mermaids in battle, and though the water sirens had been summoned by the Greek mermaid goddess Eurynome, it was hard not to wonder if there were other fair folk being lured to the dark side. They were a mischievous lot by nature, after all.

The scraping sound of the boat coming to shore sent a chill over me. I reached into my pocket and fingered my coin. If Naledi were being kept by the fey, I was going to need backup.

A disheartened huff gave me pause, stirring my curiosity, and I decided that I should at least get a glimpse of who I was up against. I peeked around the side of the hill.

Two figures sat in the boat, which I could now tell was a canoe. The smaller of the two appeared to be a young girl—a soul. With her dark hair coiled into a bun and her frilly, tulle skirt, she looked like a tiny ballerina. As the mist thinned, her skin took on a blue sheen.

The taller woman in the back of the canoe sat with a rigid back, folded arms, and a deep crease of a mouth. Her hair rose up in a great wave of glittery, red curls, tangled through with bits of grass and flowers. A crown of dewy twigs dotted with flower buds rested just above her brow, and as I stared at it, I noticed how it moved with living things—butterflies, crickets, and even a small garter snake. Her white dress clung to her body, almost disappearing into her pale skin.

"She was supposed to be waiting for us," the faerie queen said, following it up with another huff.

"Patience, Una," the girl replied, folding her hands in her lap delicately. "I feel her nearby."

The faerie queen stood and peered through the fading mist. I gasped and snapped my head back behind the hill.

"Reveal yourself, little Death. We do not have all night," the girl called out.

I wrapped my hand around the heavy throne coin and clenched my teeth. The girl was not Naledi, and I had already brought Winston an original believer. Was it really worth risking my neck for another? Still, it vexed me, not knowing who was behind this wild hunt. Not knowing who had snatched Naledi.

"He lied to us." The faerie queen snorted. The boat crunched against the shore again as if they were preparing to push off, back into the sea.

"Wait," I said, slipping out from behind the hill. "Who told you I would be here?"

The soul sighed with relief and smiled. "Let's just say it was a not so little bird, shall we?" She stood and stepped out of the boat, earning a startled gasp from her companion.

"Morgan, my sweet fawn," the queen crooned. "Promise you'll return to us."

"Of course, Una. Cross my heart." The girl, Morgan, reached back to take the queen's hands in hers. "I'll be back in time for the solstice."

I took a step closer. "You're coming with me?" I asked, confusion soaking my mind. "I don't understand. How did you even know I was here?"

"She already told you," the queen snapped. "It was the bird."

"Una, please." Morgan patted her hand. "Keep a wary eye to the sea in my absence."

The queen nodded and pressed her lips together tightly as her chin began to tremble. She released Morgan's hands so she could reach behind her wild mess of hair and untie a leather cord knotted through a hollow stone. She fastened it around the girl's neck.

"Thank you, old friend," Morgan said softly, cradling the rock in her small hands.

"Be well," the queen said.

Morgan turned to face me and lifted her chin. "I am ready."

I didn't want to test my luck by asking a third time who had sent them—at least not in front of the moody queen.

There would be plenty of time to figure out what the hell was going on once we were in the throne realm.

I gave the queen a curt nod as I rested my hand on Morgan's shoulder and tossed my coin into the air.

The sky rippled and grew brighter, and suburban turf stretched up around our feet as the sand and rock disappeared. Winston's familiar cottage came into sight, zooming in closer to us than the island. On the front porch stood Maalik.

CHAPTER TWELVE

*"Peace is not absence of conflict, it is the ability
to handle conflict by peaceful means."*
—Ronald Reagan

Original believers were remarkably wise, in my experience. Well, maybe not so much in Winston's case, but he was only a restorer of faith, not a true original believer, so he didn't really count.

Morgan was quick to recognize my shock at Maalik's presence. She fingered her stone necklace and tossed me a wary glance before vanishing into thin air.

"I'm still here," she whispered. "I'll wait for your signal before revealing myself."

"Good idea," I said under my breath.

Maalik knocked on the front door of the cottage, and from the impatient sigh that slumped his shoulders, I could tell it probably wasn't his first attempt to summon Winston. He looked the same as before, except his dark curls were pulled into a low ponytail that trailed down the back of his robe, disappearing beneath the fold of his wings. It was a formal look that he didn't seem to stray from lately, and if not for the wings and warmer shade of his skin, he could have easily passed as a reaper.

I crossed the lawn slowly, not wanting to startle him into blasting me with hellfire. What I really wanted to do was coin myself right the hell out of there, but I didn't know of a safer place to take Morgan. Besides, I was curious what Maalik was doing in the throne realm, and whether or not Winston had cracked like a rotten egg and spilled to the only other person he could.

Maalik's eyes fell on me before I'd made it halfway across the lawn. His wings shot out, expanding in a quick burst of surprise before tucking back into place. He walked down the front steps of the porch and came out to meet me, his face hardening into a neutral expression.

"What are you doing here?" he asked sharply. His eyes darted behind me for a brief second, and I wondered if he could sense Morgan or if he was just as paranoid as I was at the thought of Grim catching us here.

"I could ask you the same thing," I said, keeping my eyes focused on his.

"You shouldn't have come. You know Grim visits more frequently during the week of the Oracle Ball."

"Then why are you here? Aren't you afraid of getting busted, too?" I arched an eyebrow.

The muscles along Maalik's jaw flexed. He was just as annoyed with me as ever, and I couldn't have cared less. He let out a frustrated sigh and leaned in closer, forcing me to look up at him.

"I'm here to cover your ass," he hissed. "You're being reckless, and someone has to do damage control if you'd like your head to remain on your shoulders."

I took a step back and folded my arms. "I have no idea what you're talking about."

Maalik reached into the pocket of his robe and pulled out a wooden box. He pried off the lid with one hand, revealing a stack of incense cones. He shook the box at me, like that would somehow further prove his point. I gave him a reproachful look, wondering if maybe he was losing his mind.

"You reeked of the throne realm this afternoon," he finally said, realizing that I didn't grasp the meaning of the incense. "And you were ignorant enough to parade through Grim's office in such a state. I have to dispose of the fragrance and replace it before Grim arrives and puts two and two together."

I sighed and shook my head. "Only you would go to such extreme measures. There have to be at least four shops in the city that carry that incense."

He put the lid back on the box and frowned at me. "It is too familiar to this realm. The soul burns it daily."

I smirked. "And how would you know that?"

Maalik's face hardened again. He turned and headed back toward the cottage. "Go home, Lana."

Before he made it to the porch, the front door burst open and Winston rushed out into the yard, throwing himself at my feet.

"I'm so sorry!" he wailed. "Please forgive me. I'll do anything. *Anything.*" It was a popular promise lately.

"Well, for starters," I said, pulling my leg out of his grasp. "You can keep your stinky ashes to yourself."

Maalik's wings shifted again, fluttering anxiously. "Lana was just leaving, and I can't stay long either." He turned in a nervous circle, glancing out over the wide lawn.

Winston coiled in tighter against my legs. His eyes were dilated and wet with unshed tears. "Did you find her?" he asked.

I froze and lifted my gaze to Maalik.

The angel's brow dipped into a wrathful line. "Who?"

Winston flinched as if the fact that we weren't alone had completely escaped him. The kid was impossible, and his love-induced stupidity was likely to get us both killed.

"Who?" Maalik asked again, his voice louder. He clenched his fists at his sides.

Winston was quiet for a change. He stared up at me expectantly, letting me know that it was my decision as to what we shared with the Keeper of Hellfire.

It was at that moment when the priest soul I'd collected decided to storm out onto the porch.

"This is preposterous," he shouted, waving his bound hands in the air. His face was so red that it almost hid the blue tint of his aura.

"I thought I untied him," I said, stealing a quick glance at Winston.

"You did, but he kept trying to leave." Winston shrugged.

"Who is this?" Maalik looked like he had swallowed a wasp. He blinked stiffly and pressed his palms to his temples. When Morgan appeared beside me, I thought he might brain himself with his bare hands.

I sighed and folded my arms. "You were supposed to wait for my signal."

"I feared you had forgotten," she said innocently, but the mischievous glint in her eyes was unmistakable. She was definitely one with the fey.

Smokey hellfire swirled in Maalik's eyes, and I lifted my hands in surrender. "There's a perfectly good explanation for all of this… I'm just a little fuzzy on some of the details," I said.

"You're killing me, Lana." Maalik's hands dragged down his face, pulling at the skin until red half-moons appeared under his eyeballs.

I groaned. "Dammit, Winston. This is all your fault."

"I'll do anything," he said again, mumbling it like an addict's mantra.

Morgan glanced from me to Maalik, and then she stepped forward and curtseyed to the angel. "I'm Morgan of the fey," she announced before glancing up at the priest on the porch and adding, "here of my own free will."

Maalik's chest puffed out, and he released his skull from his death grip. He pointed a finger at the cottage. "Everyone inside. Now." His fiery eyes locked on mine. "I will not be implicated in this mess you've created," he spat.

"You think this was my doing?" I looked down at Winston and yanked my leg away again. "Thanks a lot."

"You didn't find her," he wailed. "You said you'd find her."

Maalik cleared his throat and thrust his finger at the cottage again. Before Winston could break down into one of his tantrums, I pinched his ear and dragged him up the front steps. Morgan trailed behind us.

As soon as we were inside, the priest held his bound hands out to me. I was thankful for the distraction. I could feel Maalik's eyes boring through my back as I worked on the knotted rope.

"I guess the hellcat's out of the bag now, so there's no sense holding anything back," I said, stealing a glance over my shoulder at the fuming angel.

Winston had curled up in the corner under the empty incense burner and was rocking himself into a coma. He was useless at this point, and it was only a matter of time before Grim showed up and realized what the hell was going on. And then I'd be toast. If anyone could help me out of this mess, it was Maalik.

I found listing off the disasters was easier to do without having to make eye contact.

"Winston's not an original believer," I began, taking a trembling breath after the confession. "He started losing his hold on the throne pretty quickly, and I had to find a backup soul—since it would have probably taken Grim another thousand years to get around to it."

I finished untying the priest and turned around to assess how much trouble I was in.

Maalik nodded at Morgan and the priest. "So, these are backups?"

"Sort of." I gave him a half shrug. "I guess?"

"What do you mean, you guess?"

"Well, I suppose they'll work if we can't find the throne soul," I said. "Winston lost her."

"She was taken," Winston said hollowly.

"Wait, what?" Maalik shook his head. "Winston's not the throne soul?"

"No," I huffed. "He traded places with the first backup I brought him last summer. Grim doesn't even know. That's probably the only reason I'm still alive."

Maalik sucked in a few panicked breaths. "So, the *real* throne soul is *missing*?" He paced back and forth in the foyer, his wings twitching rapidly. "Can't we just put one of these souls on the throne in the meantime?"

"No." Winston stirred in the corner. His wet eyes refocused long enough to stake us with a hopeless gaze. "The throne hasn't been abandoned. It still rests within Naledi. It's not anchored to this realm, it's anchored to her soul."

"So, basically, we're screwed?" I gawped at him. "Great."

Maalik threw his hands into the air. "Well, I guess you don't have to worry about hunting down any more souls. It's going to be hard enough hiding these two from Grim as it is."

My shoulders stiffened, and before I could relax, Maalik noticed.

"What else?" he asked, grabbing his hips with both hands.

"I wasn't actually looking for backups when I found these two." I chewed my bottom lip, trying to decide the best way to keep Horus out of the equation. There was no way Maalik would be able to let his involvement slide.

"Naledi is wearing a tracking bracelet. I was trying to locate her," I said.

Maalik's eyebrows shot up hopefully, but I shook my head.

"The tracking device only seems to work when it wants to, and every time I follow the coordinates it spits out, I find an original believer. Just not the one I'm looking for."

Maalik growled and turned in a circle before slapping a hand to the stone wall. "Perfect. It's only a matter of time before Grim pays Winston a visit." He pointed at the cowering soul. "How exactly do you suppose he'll hold up under interrogation?"

The scenario wasn't one I wanted to think about. I had enough nightmares featuring the boss man. A chill sent a shiver through my shoulders, and I hugged myself. "You said anything. Right, Winston?"

Winston's eyes welled with tears. "Anything," he whispered. "Anything."

"Good. Get up and go put some tea on for your guests. Then make up two rooms."

"And take a shower," Maalik added. "Grim will be visiting soon, and you'll want to be presentable."

Winston pulled himself off the floor and shuffled toward the kitchen, but the dead zombie stare hadn't left his eyes.

I grabbed his shoulder as he passed. "If you ever want to see Naledi again, you better start practicing your poker face."

Winston didn't move. His comatose psyche was beginning to unnerve me. I squeezed his arm until he grunted, and his eyes rolled around to meet mine.

"I will find her," I said. "But you have to buy me some time. If you can't convince Grim that everything is all right, I'll be too dead to help you. Understand?"

Something that I prayed was intelligent thought flickered through his eyes. He gave me a slow nod. My hand fell away, and he disappeared into the kitchen.

I turned back to Maalik, hoping for some sort of reassurance, but his crestfallen gaze had migrated to the two new souls. They stood side by side, silently observing the cottage, each other, and us.

A perplexed frown cut across Maalik's face. "Why do you suppose your tracking device led you to two original believers? I mean, that can't be a coincidence, right?" His suspicious eyes narrowed on me.

"I admit, it's curious," I said, rubbing my chin. "The priest was tied up when I found him, and he seemed to think it was the work of a demon."

The priest nodded vigorously. "Indeed. Who else would be capable of such violence against a servant of the Lord?" His face flushed. "Well, besides that adolescent prat you left me with." He sniffed and lifted his nose in the air.

I pointed to Morgan. "And this one claims a little bird told her I was coming to collect her."

"A *not so little* bird," she corrected me.

I raised an eyebrow. "What exactly did this bird say that made you so willing to come with me?"

"That my cooperation could save my people from the fallout of Eternity's demise."

Maalik shook his head. "It doesn't make any sense."

"And it does us no good," I said. "Not if we can't access the throne."

"Still…" Maalik stepped in front of the priest. "If the rebels have the throne soul and managed to force her to talk, it would make sense for them to gather up any other original believers they could find. Even if only to milk them of their power. This is probably the safest hiding place in all of Eternity."

The priest swallowed, and his cheeks flushed. "This is hardly the heavenly abode I was promised."

Maalik tilted his head. "Where exactly did you find this one, Lana?"

"Tartarus." My throat tightened. "Near the ruins of Beelzebub's summer manor."

Maalik's shoulders tensed, but he didn't look at me.

"The Lord of the Flies?" The priest gasped.

Maalik nodded sternly. "You don't want to end up there again, do you?"

"N-no." He knotted his hands in his robe. "This is fine. Really."

Morgan's amused smile drooped, and her brow creased.

"It's not forever," I said, feeling guilty for Maalik's fearmongering tactics. "Just until we find Naledi and get this all sorted out."

Maalik gave me a berating look. "Time to go." He snatched my elbow and yanked me toward the front door.

"Enjoy your tea," I shouted over my shoulder as Maalik slammed the panel behind us. He pulled me out into the lawn where Winston's special coins could be used.

Maalik stopped suddenly and turned around, and since he was still dragging me along, I ended up plowing right into him. My forehead collided with his chin, and we both winced.

"Owww." I tugged my arm out of his grasp so I could rub the throbbing spot above my left eyebrow. "Don't be a jerk. This is so not my fault."

He held his hand out. "I don't know how you came by it, but I'll take that tracking device now."

"Who died and made you God?" I glared at him.

"Give it to me, Lana."

"No." I took a step back and massaged the arm he had manhandled. "You don't even know how it works."

"You're going to show me," he said, shaking his outstretched hand in my face again.

I pushed it away. "Good luck with that."

To be honest, the thought of turning over the tracking device and washing my hands of the whole mess sounded fantastic. But I'd promised Winston I would find Naledi, and despite the kid's obnoxious attitude lately, I couldn't bring myself to break that promise. Plus, I hated it when Maalik bossed me around. Resisting his jerky demands was almost a necessity at this point.

"Lana," he growled through clenched teeth. "This is not a game."

"Really? And I've been having so much fun." I snorted and turned to walk away, but he grabbed my arm again, reeling me back to him.

"I don't want to threaten you," he hissed.

"Then don't."

"But I will if you force me to."

I took my free hand and placed it against his chest. My anger flared to life, and I felt heat bubble up through my center and spill down my arm. Maalik must have noticed it too because the expression on his face shifted from anger to terror. I gasped and pulled away from him. He let me go this time.

My heart punched against my ribcage, and I thought I might vomit. The last time I'd lost myself so completely had been when Craig Hogan was trying to beat me to death in an alley. My hand had melted through his chest, and I had pulled him inside out. Undoing his very existence.

I was furious with Maalik, but he was still one of the good guys. He didn't deserve that kind of wrath, least of all from me. I could still feel heat radiating through my body, but it was more from humiliation now than rage.

Maalik took another careful step away from me. "What was *that?*" he whispered. A deep sadness coated his words.

"Nothing." I couldn't even look at him. "I'm sorry."

"Right." His wings fluttered. "You're *clearly* strong enough to manage this on your own. But I don't think you should."

"Okay."

"Okay?" His eyes widened. "Just like that?"

"Yeah. Okay." I shrugged. I wanted to suggest that my compliance was a result of his milder tone and not because I felt guilty for almost unleashing my murderous rage, but I didn't. We both knew better.

I finally found the nerve to look up at him. "I'll call you the next time I'm paged."

"Thanks." He gave me a strained smile.

I nodded and flipped my coin, ready to be anywhere but there.

CHAPTER THIRTEEN

"I like coffee because it gives me the
illusion that I might be awake."
—Lewis Black

It was well after midnight by the time I stepped out of the travel booth near Holly House. After the sunshine of the throne realm, I was practically blinded by the sudden darkness. I yawned and sleepwalked myself to the condo, where I promptly fell face-first into bed.

After a whole four hours of sleep, I woke up feeling like someone had glued my eyelids shut and poured battery acid down my throat. The only thing motivating me to peel myself off the bed was the heady smell of dark coffee seeping through my bedroom door.

I dragged my feet down the hallway, groaning like one of the Evil Dead. Jenni sat at the breakfast bar in the kitchen. She was still in her silk bathrobe, which was odd at this hour, considering how early she usually went in to work. Her hair was knotted up in a messy bun, but her eyes looked brighter than I'd seen them in a long time. Amazing what a full night of sleep could do.

She rolled her eyes at my zombie imitation and nodded to a fresh cup of coffee on the bar next to her. I snagged it up and took a long drink before climbing onto a barstool.

"Marry me," I said, pressing the mug to my chest with both hands. I breathed in the exotic steam and closed my eyes, sighing dreamily.

Jenni snorted. "It's too early for proposals, and I don't swing your way."

"I wasn't talking to you," I said, petting the coffee mug.

She twisted in her barstool and rested an elbow on the counter. "Must be slim pickings out there."

"Ha. Like I'd know anything about that." Dating was a thing of the past—and not just because I wasn't over my undercover ex. Relationships took time and trust, and both were in short supply.

"How was your talk with Kevin?" Jenni asked, pressing the back of her hand over her mouth as she yawned.

I glared at her and slurped my coffee.

"Went over that well, huh?"

"Like a hand grenade."

I half expected to find Kevin in his room now that I'd relieved him of his supply. But I should have known better. He'd probably be after another fix until his savings ran out. As his mentor, I was a signer on his accounts. I could always freeze his funds until he got his shit together, but I'd heard too many horror stories about what addicts were willing to do for a bump, and I didn't want to be responsible for any of it.

I grumbled and stood to refill my cup. Jenni held out her mug, and I topped hers off, too.

"So, are you taking the day off?" I asked, trying to spin the conversation in a more pleasant direction.

"I wish." Her nose scrunched up resentfully. "I'm going in late. Grim wants me at the big safety meeting for the ball."

That meant the entire council would be at Reapers Inc. this morning—none of whom I was eager to see.

"Super." I squeezed my eyes shut and groaned.

Jenni grinned. "It's at seven, so if you hurry, you might make it in and out before the council arrives." She stood and drained her coffee before heading off to get ready.

I sat at the bar a minute longer, grumbling over my mug. As if work didn't suck enough without having to go in early. I debated going in late instead, after the meeting had already started, but knowing my luck, it would probably let out just in time for me to end up riding an elevator down with the entire council. That was an unnerving thought, and just the motivation I needed to hop my ass up and make for the shower.

I didn't waste time drying my hair, but I did slick a handful of gel through my short curls so they wouldn't frizz. Then I quickly pulled on my robe over my standard workwear—a black, long-sleeved shirt, jeans, and the dark gray boots Josie had helped me pick out with the bonus we'd received for bringing in Winston.

Jenni was shrugging into a blazer when I reemerged in the kitchen to feed Saul. His sad, droopy ears perked slightly, but he ate with less vigor than usual. I was hoping his mood would improve once Coreen returned from Olympus, which reminded me that I still needed to find homes for two of her pups.

"I thought you said seven." I gave Jenni a confused look.

She nodded. "I did. I have to pick up donuts and set up the conference room."

Fetching donuts seemed like a pretty menial task for someone of Jenni's rank, but Grim probably didn't trust anyone else to oversee things at the council headquarters. There were spies on both sides of the war, and we had enough disadvantages as it was.

Jenni tugged the cuffs of her white dress shirt down before rolling them up with the arms of her blazer. Then she draped her messenger bag and sheathed katana over her head and shoulders, letting the straps hang diagonally across her chest. She skipped the traditional robe, but I knew she kept several in her office.

"A donut doesn't sound half bad," I said, grabbing my bag and a knit scarf out of the coat closet. I ruffled Saul's ears and scratched under his chin before following Jenni out of the condo.

Limbo City was a tiny island, so while Holly House and Reapers Inc. were on completely opposite sides, it was only a six-block walk. On most days, I was still inclined to take the travel booths. Maybe it was all the overtime wearing on me, or maybe the convenience was just too tempting. Perhaps I was getting lazy.

Jenni never used the booths. This morning was no different. She turned right once we passed the front gate of Holly House, heading east along Divine Boulevard. I shot a longing gaze at the travel booth in the opposite direction and followed her down to Market Street.

The sound of the morning tide greeted us as we neared the sea. The Three Fates Factory pumps churned in the distance, noisily sucking up the soul-infused waters. A handful of vendors were setting up in the market area just before the harbor, but the tents and tables were spread thinner than usual. A few sloppy, red blotches dotted the empty spaces where the Nephilim Guard had tried to scrub away rebel paint.

The donut shop was farther up Market Street. The smell of buttery pastries and frosting mingling with fresh coffee grew stronger when we passed the harbor. My mouth watered as we joined the small crowd of reapers, nephilim, and souls gathered under the shop's white awning.

Nessa, the tiny, Scottish brownie who ran the shop, stood atop a counter just inside a sliding window. For barely two feet tall, her presence was quite commanding. She read off tickets and collected coins as two nephilim in white aprons ran back and forth behind her, dishing out donuts tucked in wax paper and steaming cups of coffee just as fast as their little fey boss could shout orders.

"Ms. Fang, good day to you," Nessa hollered upon spotting Jenni. She snatched a ticket off a spinning rack and waved it at her feathered bakers. "Grim's lassie is here for pickup!"

Hungry, resentful eyes glanced our way, but Jenni ignored them. She handed Nessa a coin and took a large, white box from one of the bakers. Shiny glazes and bright sprinkles could be seen through a clear plastic window on the lid.

I waved my hand before Nessa turned away. "Could I get a couple of those amazing bear claws I smell?" I gave her my most innocent smile and prayed none of the other customers would make a fuss.

Nessa put a hand on her bony hip and smirked at me. "Aye, lass. But I wouldn't rely on yer flattery to get you through the whole day."

She snapped her fingers, and one of the bakers leaned through the open window to hand me a paper sack with my pastries. I gave Nessa a coin with enough left over for a nice tip and quickly moved out of the way as a pair of guards stepped up to collect their breakfast.

Jenni snickered as we cut west down Council Street. "She's right, you know? I definitely don't think Grim would appreciate flattery. Especially not from you."

I took a bite out of a bear claw and grinned at her. "What a lovely tie, sir. Black is most definitely the new black. And it goes so well with your dazzling scowl. However do you pull it off?" I batted my eyelashes.

Jenni snorted. "I'd pay to see that."

"How much?"

"Not enough to cover any more of the rent, so you probably shouldn't." Her smile tapered off as we passed the city park, and we both fell silent.

The tall hedge hid the memorial statues and Josie's bench, but the tulip trees that circled the sacred spot had begun to change color. A golden canopy stood out among shorter, red-leafed trees, marking the resting place of our fallen. The brittle foliage crackled as the wind pushed against my face, cold and scathing, and I realized that I was holding my breath.

I'd known plenty of superstitious humans who thought it appropriate to hold their breath when passing a graveyard. A common theory for this was that breathing would invite an evil spirit to possess their soul. Others suggested that it should be done out of respect for the dead since they could no longer breathe themselves. It seemed ridiculous to me, and yet, I found myself doing it every time I passed the memorials.

I cleared my throat as we crossed Destiny Avenue, leaving the park behind. "How's the rebel lair search going?"

Jenni tucked the donut box in the crook of one arm so she could swipe her bangs out of her face before frowning at me. I wasn't supposed to ask these kinds of questions, but from her tired expression, I knew there wasn't much to tell.

"Between the afterlives, the sea, the mortal realm, and Limbo City, the bastards are everywhere." She sighed heavily and looked away. "I haven't collected a soul in two weeks."

She sounded bothered by that fact, but it wasn't too surprising. Jenni actually liked harvesting. She had more certificates and licenses than any other reaper, and she was qualified to harvest on five continents and with any specialty unit she wanted. If that wasn't admirable enough, she was only a sixth-generation reaper. It was understandable that the older generations envied her position, but no one could deny she had earned it.

"I'd trade you places in a heartbeat," I said, then thought better of it and added, "Except for the working with Grim bit. Otherwise, I'd definitely rather be kicking some rebel ass than reaping souls."

"I'm sure you would." Her smile softened sympathetically.

"And not just because I'd like to crucify that skank who had her mitts all over Beelzebub."

"Of course not."

"I'm serious."

"Sure, I know." Jenni nodded.

Her tone was patronizing, and I felt my cheeks burn at her sorry pretense. I blew out a dismissive sigh and turned away from her, stuffing the rest of the bear claw I was working on into my mouth.

It killed me that part of Bub's cover involved seducing one of the rebels. I wasn't stupid. I knew he was bedding her, and the thought was like a sucker punch to the heart every time it crossed my mind. So at least my homicidal urges toward *her* were genuine.

I could keep Bub's big, ugly secret, but all bets were off when it came to the demonic harlot. I'd kill her the first chance I got. Trouble was, my ties to Bub made the council question my loyalty—even after I'd made the headlines for trashing his flat in Pandemonium—and Jenni hadn't included me in a special assignment for some time, not since Josie's death.

Reapers Inc. was half a block away, and I was ready to make my mad dash and get gone. If I were quick enough, maybe I could slip in an early harvest before the rest of the unit showed up to collect their dockets.

Jenni stopped suddenly and dropped the box of donuts. My head jerked up to follow her line of sight, and I nearly choked on my breakfast.

Three demons scaled the face of the Reapers Inc. building. They were a low order, garden-variety with vaguely human features. Their bald heads were horned, and their red flesh was thin and unclothed, showing sharp bones underneath. Blackened talons shot out from their fingers and toes, leaving me to wonder how they had managed to climb up the smooth glass window that overlooked the lobby. Each of the demons wielded a spray can of red paint.

Jenni's lips curled back, revealing clenched teeth. She drew her katana with a growl before taking off down the sidewalk. I didn't have my axe with me, and I was no Spiderman, but I'd be damned if I passed up an opportunity to prove my worth against the rebels.

I yanked my robe over my head and stuffed it into my bag with my remaining pastry. My fingers brushed the strap of throwing stars Bub had given me during my demon defense training. I couldn't bring myself to wear them since his betrayal, but they were too useful to leave buried in the back of my closet. I unfastened a star and hurried ahead of the small mob forming in front of Reapers Inc.

A dozen nephilim guards appeared above us, jabbing their golden spears at the rebel demons. The creatures hissed their displeasure but didn't turn to strike. They were too focused on their task.

One of the guards crept in closer and plunged his spear through a demon's back. It howled and bowed away from the window before falling to the street below, hands wrapped around the spear point poking through its ribcage.

The crowd gasped and backed away, all except for one soul—a woman with white eyes and a haunting grin. Jenni shoved her aside and plunged her katana into the demon's neck. It gurgled out its last breath as she yanked the spear free. She tossed it up to its nephilim owner before flicking the blood from her sword and turning on the strange soul.

"What's wrong with you?" she asked the woman, taking in her ancient gown and eerie eyes. "You need to back up. You could get hurt."

She refused to move. "It's a simple mark," she said, so softly I almost couldn't hear her over the murmur of the crowd. "But they're sure to get it wrong if I don't stay close."

Jenni's eyes narrowed as she pointed her katana at the woman's throat. "Call them down. Now."

"Patience. They're almost finished," she chirped.

I craned my neck up to watch the demons as they completed the top and bottom arms of a backward E. The symbol was at least twenty feet tall. Grim was going to shit a pineapple.

I pinched a corner of the throwing star in my hand and hurled it at the nearest demon. It came dangerously close to nicking a guard's wing, grazed the shoulder of the demon, and then smashed through the front window.

The glass shattered inward, buckling further from the weight of the demons as they sprang off the building like a pair of gangly toads. Grim was going to shit *two* pineapples.

Or maybe the second one could be a pinecone. I mean, at least the sign of the rebels wasn't an issue now, right?

The two demons dropped to the sidewalk. They crept toward Jenni, hissing and clicking their tongues. The guards swooped down, taking jabs at them with their spears, but the demons were oblivious. When all was said and done, they had to be pinned to the concrete like giant bugs, their guts oozing out and sizzling like frying bacon.

The woman didn't seem bothered in the least. She held out her hand, dancing it along as if she were playing with an invisible puppet on strings. A gaudy lump of a ring rested on her middle finger.

Jenni kept her sword trained on the woman as she nodded to a guard. "Cuff her and take her up to the interrogation room."

As soon as the nephilim stepped forward, a bony hand shot up through the sidewalk like an apparition, wrapping around the guard's ankle. He yelped and hopped back a step, stabbing his spear at the creepy hand as he flapped his wings, lifting up and out of reach.

Several screams ripped up from the crowd, and everyone parted again, forming a second clearing in the center of Council Street. Another demon was working its way up out of the ground. Fire licked along the asphalt as if a portal to Hell had just been opened beneath the city. Several souls and reapers took off toward the nearest travel booth.

I turned back to find Jenni and the demon puppeteer circling each other. Jenni's katana was still aimed at the woman's face, and I could tell she wanted to shish-kebob her in a bad way. Jenni's resolve was rock-solid, though I'd seen her act out of vengeance before—like the time she split Caim's skull in half like a coconut. She wouldn't do the same to the soul unless she had no other choice. Grim would want the woman for questioning.

"The ring!" I shouted, pointing at the soul's hand.

Jenni's sword moved so fast I could hardly tell what she'd done until demon lady clasped her hand to her chest. Her fingers were still intact, but blood gushed from her palm and ran down her arm to her elbow. Her chin snapped around, and she pierced me with her vacant eyes before shoving her middle finger into her mouth and sucking off the ring. Her brows cinched together as she swallowed.

"I said cuff her!" Jenni roared over the frantic crowd. "And then search the city for any more of these rodents," she added, stomping her boot down between the horns of a demon that had become stuck in the concrete once the woman removed her ring.

Two guards finally found the nerve to seize the soul, and Jenni followed them as they wrestled her inside and away from the noisy mob. Her head twisted backward at an unnatural angle, and her ghostly eyes fell on me again. She was shouting something, but I couldn't hear.

A gust of wind whooshed over the crowd, and Maalik dropped down beside me. His wings folded back sharply as he grabbed my shoulder. "Lana, are you all right?"

I nodded and shrugged his hand away. Another hiss of wings sounded over the chaos, and Ridwan, the other Islamic angel on the council, pushed through the souls and reapers clustered along the opposite side of the street. He scanned the crowd, frowning when his eyes settled on Maalik and me. So much for avoiding the council today.

Maalik looked up at the shattered window and sighed. "I feel sorry for the mongrel who desecrated Grim's sanctuary."

"Yeah, that'd be me." My throat tightened as he slowly turned horrified eyes my way. "In my defense, the glass was covered in rebel paint anyway." That didn't seem to help. "And I was aiming at a demon. And I was crucial in stopping Ms. Demon Summoner over there."

He actually looked like he was going to be sick. "Demon summoner? But that's not possible. Especially with the current travel restrictions. Unless…" His eyes grew wider.

"Nooo," I said in disbelief and shook my head. "No. Nope. Don't even think it."

Winston's coins were spelled to bypass the travel restrictions while he was still on the throne. He'd set the new rules, so of course he could bend them when he pleased. But some lady with a funky ring? That wasn't supposed to happen. That couldn't happen. Not unless the rules had changed. Or if something had happened to Naledi.

"I have to tell Grim," Maalik whispered, leaning in so close to me that I could smell his minty mouthwash.

"Like hell," I hissed under my breath and glanced nervously at the cluster of bystanders around us. "You'd be signing my death warrant, and you know it." My stomach knotted, and my heart fluttered in my chest as if looking to escape. "I just need a little more time."

Maalik gritted his teeth. "The Oracle Ball is Saturday. If we can't find her by then, we'll all be out of time."

Four days. I had four days to rescue Naledi and return her to the throne realm. Otherwise, when Grim gave the order for the soul matter distribution, Winston would have to explain how he didn't actually have any soul matter at his disposal. And then my ass was history.

"Lana." Jenni stepped over the remains of one of the speared demons. "Grim wants to see you."

"Shit." I pointed a finger at the window. "You told him that was my fault, didn't you?"

Jenni's amused demeanor from our walk was gone. She was all business now. "We're wasting time. Come on."

CHAPTER FOURTEEN

*"I truly believe the wireless mouse was invented so people
at work had one less thing to hang themselves with."*
—Mike Vanatta

The lobby was covered in shards of glass and splattered paint. I'd broken the window before it had a chance to dry. Three nephilim in grey, janitor jumpsuits swept and mopped the marble floor, grumbling under their breaths. From Ellen's freak-out over my dusty robe yesterday, I knew that the major pre-ball housecleaning had already been done, so I could hardly blame them for the dirty looks cast my way.

A handful of reapers huddled in the far back corner behind the help desk. A vase of tulips had been knocked over. The soggy flowers drooped over the edge of the counter, dripping water in a puddle on the floor, but no one seemed to notice. Every wide, accusing eye seemed to be pinned on me. Maybe I was being paranoid. The window couldn't have been that damn expensive, and I was certainly not the only one at fault here.

"Ignore them," Jenni said, pushing the elevator button.

I bit my tongue and resisted the urge to make a break for it. Nothing screamed guilty like fleeing the scene.

The elevator doors slid open, and once we were closed inside, I turned to Jenni. "I totally didn't mean to break the window. You know that, right? You'll tell Grim?"

Jenni scoffed. "Really? You think this is about the window?"

"If not that, then what?"

Jenni squinted suspiciously at me. "The soul requested you personally. She says she has a message from the rebels, but she was ordered to deliver it to you alone."

"*What?*" I gripped the railing behind me. It felt like my stomach had fallen through the floor and down the elevator shaft.

The doors opened onto the thirty-seventh floor, and I thought I might barf up my morning pastry. If we'd still been in the lobby, I would have bolted. Jenni strolled out of the car like it was just a typical day at the office.

I hadn't been to the thirty-seventh floor since last summer when we captured Loki, and Grim had invited me to his secret torture chamber to watch him work. He wanted me to know that he wasn't afraid to get his hands dirty, that the suit and desk didn't mean shit. It was a lesson I wasn't likely to forget.

The floor of horrors hadn't changed much. The lobby still looked like an ordinary office front undergoing renovations. Dusty, plastic sheeting hung from the ceiling, obscuring the area behind the receptionist desk. A tool belt was draped over a step ladder, and faint music crackled out of a radio. The only giveaway was a smear of dark blood along the unfinished floor.

Jenni paused and looked over her shoulder at me. I hadn't moved from the elevator, and I was still gripping the inside railing as if it were the only thing keeping me from being dragged to Hell.

"You've been here before," she said, surprise hitching her voice.

"Once," I rasped, trying to find my breath. All of a sudden, my scarf was too tight. I dug my fingers inside the knot and tried to loosen it.

Jenni reached into the elevator and took my hand, tugging me out into the lobby. "Don't fall apart on me, Lana. Everything is going to be fine. Okay?"

"Right." I squeezed her hand and let go, not wanting to look as vulnerable as I felt when we met with the big, bad boss.

There wasn't much time to practice my poker face, but I gave it my best. It was hard telling what demon-lady's message was or who it was from. There were so many awful possibilities, and with Grim hawk-eyeing me, I would have to be extra careful how I received the message. Khadija help me.

Jenni led the way down a long hall sectioned off with more plastic sheeting. Every few feet, a splotch of blood let me know that we were on the right path. The woman's hand clearly hadn't been a priority.

I'd never heard of a soul bleeding out. I imagined it was possible, but it seemed unlikely. Sure, a soul could be beaten or tortured, but they were pretty damn resilient. I guess they'd have to be in order to spend any amount of time in one of the hell regions.

A flutter of wings sounded from farther down the hall, and I heard Grim's gravelly voice loud and clear. "Use the shackles. Her feet, too. We're going to need more tarp."

I swallowed the bile rising in the back of my throat and tried to push away the nightmares crowding the forefront of my mind. I was just here to receive a message. Then I could leave…before Grim began dissecting the soul with needlenose pliers and a reciprocating saw.

Jenni took a sharp left down another makeshift hallway. Shortly after, she turned right and stepped through a gap in the hanging plastic. It was almost indiscernible, like a mirrored funhouse maze. I would have been lost if not for the blood trail. The smears along the floor were growing lighter, ending at the point where Jenni had disappeared. I took one last deep breath before following her in.

The room was set up the same way Loki's had been, with the soul strapped to a metal autopsy table, propped up on its end against an unfinished wall. My eyes were instantly drawn to the table beside her, the contents hidden beneath a black, leather apron.

"Captain Harvey," Grim said, his voice tinged with warning. I dragged my eyes away from the table and blinked at him as if coming out of a trance.

A nephilim guard tugged on the chain stretching between the soul's feet and stood, retreating out of the room after Grim waved him away. As soon as he was gone, Grim rotated his hand and beckoned me closer. I swallowed and took a careful step forward.

The soul's vacant eyes reached for me, and her words spilled out suddenly as if forced from her lips by magic. "His secrets are no more. Our prisoner can only be pardoned in exchange for a worthy soul, delivered to the peak marked in fool's blood, next sacred eve."

My throat went dry as I struggled to appear unmoved. Each breath was a battle, but I didn't dare speak. It was entirely possible that this was a trap and everything depended upon my next move. As long as I stood perfectly still, maybe I wouldn't fall to my imminent death.

Grim's cruel features warped as he turned on me. "What is she talking about, Lana? You must know. The message is for you." He clenched and unclenched his fists as if he were trying to keep from wrapping his hands around my neck.

"I-I don't know." My breath rushed in and out, trying to keep pace with my heartbeat. I fucking hated riddles, especially the kind that sicced my boss on me like a rabid hellhound.

Grim ground his teeth until they creaked under the pressure. "Well think, dammit." He kicked the foot of the autopsy table, and it rattled violently as it slid off the wall and rotated back into a horizontal position. The soul didn't even flinch. Her empty eyes stayed focused on me, even after Grim ripped the leather apron from the table, revealing his arsenal.

The room was suddenly a million degrees. Sweat prickled across my chest and back. I felt it soaking through my clothes.

I'd seen my share of gore, and I was no stranger to violence. But this was different. A battle of wills I could do. Put a weapon in my hands, and I'd spar with the best of them all day. There was just something entirely unnerving about torture, though. The complete helplessness. The goal of pain rather than victory.

I didn't want to see what was coming next, so I scrambled to come up with something useful, even if it was total bullshit.

"Is anyone missing? Gabriel? Kevin?" I stammered, knotting my fingers around the strap of my bag.

Jenni shook her head slowly. "Not that I'm aware of." Her eyes fell briefly on the table of horrors, but she quickly looked away, choosing instead to stare at me. "A worthy soul? What could that—?"

"Leave us," Grim snapped.

I desperately wished the order had been directed at me, but the way Jenni scrambled out of the room left no doubt that it wasn't. Her footsteps faded quickly, and a terrifying silence filled the void.

Grim's face was suddenly an inch from mine. His dark pupils bled out to fill the whites of his eyes, and his voice dropped dangerously low. "I don't give two shits about the rebels' supposed prisoner. We will not be turning over *any* soul, and if you even think to make a deal behind my back, it will be you on my table next. Do you understand?"

I nodded shakily, unable to find my next breath. My knees buckled, and it was all I could do to stay upright.

Grim twisted away from me sharply and snatched the front of the soul's robe, ripping it down the middle to expose her breasts and stomach. My insides clenched, and I looked away.

"As for you," Grim said in a deceptively lighter tone as he fingered the tools on his table, "I have a very particular method when it comes to deciphering rebel codes."

The soul's eerie smile hadn't budged. "I spent a thousand years in the eighth circle of Hell with my head twisted around backward. I wouldn't boast of your method just yet," she said.

"Is that the reason for the reversed E?" I asked.

She pressed her lips together and smiled smugly, clearly not interested in revealing the rebel's secrets.

Grim busied himself polishing a curved fishing knife. My skin crawled as I backed toward the exit. "I should go," I said quietly, almost a request.

"Of course. Lots of souls to harvest." Grim nodded, his back still turned to me. "Tell Ms. Fang to reschedule the council meeting for tomorrow morning before you scamper off."

"Yes, sir."

"And, Lana?" He looked at me over his shoulder, his pupils still swollen and inky black. "I meant what I said." The fishing knife clanked against the autopsy table next to the soul's ear, earning a small jump out of her.

"Yes, sir," I said again, trying to keep my voice even.

He watched me a moment longer, and seemingly satisfied by my shaken appearance, he turned back to the soul. As his knife lowered between her breasts, I turned and ran from the room.

I didn't care that Grim could probably hear my boots slapping against the floor. He already knew I was terrified of him, so what did it matter? I pressed my hands over my ears and didn't remove them until I reached the elevators, where I slapped at the buttons until a pair of doors finally slid open.

The buttons on the inside were harder to navigate, seeing as how my hands were trembling as if I'd just taken a stroll across Antarctica. I hesitated over the lobby button, and then remembered that I hadn't picked up my docket yet. There was also the message I was supposed to deliver to Jenni—as long as I didn't swallow my tongue first.

I pushed the button for the seventy-fifth floor, and as the car migrated up and away, I slid down the mirrored wall, shaking as the adrenaline fizzled out of my system.

My mind calmed slowly, but as it did, the soul's riddle came back to me.

"His secrets are no more. Our prisoner can only be pardoned in exchange for a worthy soul, delivered to the peak marked in fool's blood, next sacred eve."

Beelzebub. It had to be. And the rebels wanted to trade him for the throne soul. But didn't they already have the throne soul? Had Naledi convinced them otherwise? Or had someone else nabbed her? This was a fine fucking mess.

A peak marked in fool's blood didn't give me much to go on either, but as for the next sacred eve, that could only mean the night before the ball. Why were all my damn deadlines stacking up so closely together? Talk about unfair.

The fact that I was expected to achieve the impossible just added insult to injury. My best bet at this point was to take the elevator up one more level and throw myself off the roof.

CHAPTER FIFTEEN

"All discarded lovers should be given a second chance,
but with somebody else."
—Mae West

A hush fell over the office as I stepped off the elevator, and a dozen reapers turned to stare me down as if they'd just placed bets on my life expectancy. I was clearly the water-cooler topic of the day. Lucky me.

Paul Brom, the captain of the Recovery Unit, politely tipped his bowler hat in my direction before backing into the vacated elevator. A few others quickly followed, doing their best not to make eye contact with me.

Adrianna Bates, the captain of the Mother Goose Unit and Josie's former mentor, stood her ground in the doorway of the break room, casting me a reproachful look over the top of her coffee mug. She hadn't said two words to me since Josie's memorial, but it didn't take a psychic to tell me that she held me responsible. And some days, I still felt I was.

Ellen gave me a pained smile as she handed over my docket. "Here you go, sweetie," she whispered, sliding a foil-wrapped truffle across her desk. "You look like you could use a pick-me-up."

"Thanks." I couldn't even muster a smile. "Is Jenni in her office?"

Ellen nodded, and when I turned to head down the hall, everyone besides Adrianna shuffled around, trying to look busy. I entered Jenni's office without knocking and quickly closed the door behind me.

"Is everything all right?" Jenni shot up from her chair.

"No, it most definitely is not." I flopped down onto one of the leather benches in front of her desk and hissed out an agitated breath. "I should have called in sick today."

Jenni folded her arms and regarded me with annoyed disdain. "Well, I'm no doctor, and I have a lot to juggle right now. So…"

I gaped at her. "Seriously? You just left me alone with that monster in his evil lair, and you're put out with *me?*"

Her cheeks puffed out, and she rolled her eyes, but I could tell the jab inspired at least a smidge of guilt. "Sorry. Boss's orders. What do you need?" she asked, sitting back down.

I stuck my bottom lip out and tilted my head as if considering whether or not to accept her apology. Since my fight or flight response was still leaning heavily toward the latter, I decided it would do.

"Grim said to tell you to reschedule the council meeting for tomorrow morning."

"Already done." She propped her elbows on the desk and tapped her fingertips together under her chin. "I didn't land this job by way of my good looks."

"Great. Guess I can get to scampering then." I gave Jenni a callous grin and stood to leave.

The humor drained from her face as she hopped up to cut me off. "Did you learn any more about the message?"

I felt my brows draw together and struggled to keep a neutral expression as I shook my head. Jenni didn't look convinced.

"You'd tell me if something came to you, right?" Her eyes roved over my face desperately. I nodded and reached for the door, but she pressed a fist across the jamb. "You can trust me, Lana. I work for Grim, same as you, but that doesn't mean he owns me."

"I know that," I said, laughing nervously and tugging at the doorknob. "Of course I trust you."

She moved her hand and let me open the door. Quick footsteps echoed down the hall. When had everyone become so damn nosy? I swallowed my next words and turned to face Jenni.

"Wanna do donuts again tomorrow?" I asked, trying to ease the sour look on her face. Her brows dropped lower.

"Maybe I'll actually get to eat one this time," she grumbled. "Damn mob trampled that box into a puddle of sugary mush."

I grinned and stuck my hand down into my bag, retrieving the second bear claw I'd stashed there. Jenni's face lit as I handed it to her.

"I might make it through today without killing anyone, after all." She waved the pastry at me in thanks before taking a bite and heading back to her desk.

I slipped through the office without crossing anyone else's path and gave Ellen a silent salute as I entered an elevator. My day seemed to be back on schedule, and as shaken as I was, I needed a dose of normal to balance my psyche.

My mind was still running laps around the thought of Bub being a rebel prisoner. Maybe it was a trap. Perhaps he was just fine, and this was a cutthroat attempt to trick me into playing for the wrong team. Of course, after Grim's encore performance in the torture room, I was really struggling with the idea of good and evil. Was it really all for the sake of peace? Or did some part of him actually delight in the appalling *work* he was doing?

The elevator came to a stop on the seventy-third floor, and I smothered a groan. *This* was why I had done the flight of the bumblebee getting ready this morning. I had wanted to avoid being trapped in a tight space with a member of the council.

The doors slid open, revealing Maalik standing alone in the hall. His wings fluttered eagerly and then folded back as he stepped inside. "I was hoping I'd catch you."

I sneered at him. "Enjoy it while it lasts. After Saturday, you might not be so lucky."

The skin around Maalik's eyes tightened, but he kept his smile in place and darted his eyes up at the corner of the elevator. A little red light blinked down on us, a reminder that we were being watched.

Maalik laughed softly as if I'd just made a joke. A silvery feather shook loose from his wings and drifted up against the back wall of the car, where a dozen smaller, white nephilim feathers had collected. It was a curious problem since the Guard became a thing. The janitors probably swept up enough down each week to run a successful pillow company on the side.

When the elevator opened on the lobby, I rushed out ahead of Maalik. The marble floor was clean again, and the jagged edges of glass had been removed from the frame of the front window, but a new pane hadn't been installed yet. The cold autumn air blew through the lobby, making the tulips pucker. The Roman goddess Flora, Limbo City's resident florist, dashed from vase to vase, placing little baggies over the buds to postpone their wilting.

"Slow down," Maalik hissed in my ear as he caught up to me. "I need a word with you."

"Duty calls," I chirped, waving my soul docket at him.

He snatched my elbow as we passed through the front doors and onto the sidewalk. "I'm coming with you."

"Right." I laughed.

"I'll make myself useful," he insisted. I gave him a sober glance, realizing he was serious.

"Absolutely not. An angel shadowing me on the job? That's the most ridiculous thing I've ever heard."

Maalik sighed. "Grim has requested that I tail you, to make sure you don't do anything moronic. *His* words, not mine," he quickly added, feeling the weight of my death glare.

"I don't need a babysitter."

"You do if you intend to trade the throne soul for your treacherous lover," he said under his breath, raising an eyebrow in challenge when I gasped.

"Because Armageddon sounds like such a swell honeymoon," I said with an offended snort.

"Maybe not…but I don't hear you denying that you still love him." A sad, pitying look crossed his face, and I felt my skin tingle with wrath.

I wanted to scream, but I bit my tongue and swallowed my temper before stepping in close to him, pointing my nose up at his. "So what if I do?"

The pity shifted to arrogance. "And this is why you can't be trusted alone."

I rolled my eyes and let out a frustrated growl as I stepped away from him, taking off toward the harbor. If he wanted to tag along, he was going to get a workout.

Maalik didn't give up easily. His gait was strong, and he managed to keep up without breaking a sweat. "You know, if you would turn over the tracking device, I'd be more than happy to leave you alone," he said casually.

"You wish, jerk." How stupid did he think I was?

His wing brushed my arm as he took flight for a brief second and landed right in my path. I staggered to a halt and threw my hands down at my sides. "Make yourself useful, huh?"

Maalik folded his arms over his chest, and the beginnings of hellfire swirled in his eyes. "I'll have that device by the end of the day, Lana. Or else our truce is void. I'll tell Grim everything I know."

"You wouldn't." All the air left my lungs, and I could barely speak around the lump in my throat.

Maalik looked apologetic, but he refused to take back his threat. "You may love whomever you choose to, but I will not lend a hand in the undoing of Eternity through omission."

The self-righteous bastard. Maalik hadn't trusted me when we were an item, so I didn't know why I expected him to now. Still, it stung to be treated like a threat after everything I'd been through and done for Eternity.

I swallowed and gave him a stiff nod, blinking back unshed tears. "I left it on the ship," I lied. "Follow me to the harbor, and it's yours."

Maalik reached for my shoulder, but I recoiled in disgust. He tucked his hand against his chest as if I'd burned him. "It's for the best," he said softly, as though he were trying to convince himself rather than me.

"Whatever." I stepped around him and continued on toward the harbor.

I was tempted to take the travel booth on the corner of Destiny Avenue if only to shave off five more minutes of the painfully awkward encounter, but I needed the extra time to think.

I was really getting sick of the blackmail game. Horus was one thing, but I'd really thought I could trust Winston and Maalik. Seeing how quickly they were willing to throw me under the bus to get their way was difficult to process, and it hurt something in me that I wasn't sure could be mended, even while it filled me with a trembling relief. Some of my secrets were still mine alone, and they'd be staying that way now. I'd learned my lesson.

My unit was waiting on deck when I arrived with Maalik. The angel drew plenty of suspicious eyes, but no one questioned his presence—not even Kevin, who I was beyond surprised to see.

My apprentice leaned against the deck railing, shivering as he hugged himself. I wondered if the wrinkled robe he wore was the same one I'd seen him in the night before. His curls were a frizzy mess, and his eyes were dark and sunken, following Maalik and me wrathfully as we cut across the deck.

"I'll be right back," I said, waving my hand at the gang in casual greeting.

Maalik followed me down the back hall to the new captain's cabin Kevin had remodeled for me before his downward spiral. The room was a dream, all billowy white curtains and bedding, surrounded by glossy wood. The French doors and oval windows were masterfully detailed. It made my heart hurt, thinking of the last night I'd spent here with Bub.

"I'll be right back," I said to Maalik, before stepping inside the tiny bathroom in the corner of the cabin and shutting the door.

There was an oval window above the toilet, and my pulse quickened at the thought of slipping through it, leaping down to the dock, and coining off. Anywhere would do. Still, I had four days left before going on the lam would be a necessity. A lot could change in that time.

I sighed and pulled the tracking compact out of my pocket. It hadn't really done me much good. The two new souls couldn't take Naledi's place on the throne, and if the rebels were demanding that I deliver her, then she couldn't be in *too* much danger. Right?

I knew Maalik wouldn't wait forever, and with each second that passed, my heart picked up speed. The compact was heavy in my hands. I couldn't still my mind enough to think of a reasonable way to keep the thing from him, but that didn't mean I had to give him the rest of the bracelets tucked inside.

I opened the lid and dumped the remaining five ivory bracelets into my hand. They were linked to the tracking device, but they wouldn't activate until placed on a soul. I stuffed them into my pocket and snapped the compact lid shut before flushing the toilet and opening the bathroom door.

Maalik stood just outside with his hand lifted, prepared to knock.

"Worried I'd make a break for it?" I snorted and flipped the compact at him.

He fumbled with the device, and his wings gave a nervous flutter as he clutched it to his chest. Then he turned it around in his hands carefully. "How does it work?"

I shrugged. "Read a book. I have a unit to run since, apparently, I can still be trusted to do *that*."

He gave me a frustrated sigh before an uneasy frown crossed his face. "If the rebels are demanding the throne soul, then they can't possibly have her."

I folded my arms. "Who does that leave?"

"I don't know." He pressed his lips together thoughtfully.

"Well, I'd love to stay and help solve the world's problems, but you've made it pretty clear that I'm not qualified." I walked across the room and opened the cabin door, holding it open for him.

Maalik's wings ruffled with annoyance. He stalked past me, only turning back for a brief second to give me a scolding glance. "Thank you for cooperating."

I batted my lashes and threw a hand to my chest in furious mockery. "Oh, my pleasure. You know me. Just can't resist the blackmail threats."

I slammed the cabin door in his baffled face and didn't come out until the beating of his wings had faded into the distance.

CHAPTER SIXTEEN

"Fear is the path to the dark side. Fear leads to anger.
Anger leads to hate. Hate leads to suffering."
—Yoda

Since it was only Tuesday, there wasn't much I could do except worry myself sick about Bub. At least until Friday night. That sounded like buckets of fun. It was a good thing I was so adept at distracting myself. I'd been doing a lot of that lately, and it helped that I had a heap of souls to harvest.

Kevin's startling appearance took my mind off things for a while, too. In addition to looking like the walking dead, he had developed a few annoying ticks. Every so often, his right eye twitched spastically, like a Venus flytrap that had bitten off more than it could chew. And late October was chilly, but the way his teeth violently chattered was a little uncalled for.

"You sure you're up for this?" I asked him as we walked through a mortal hospital. A few dozen burn victims from a hotel fire were being wheeled in on gurneys.

Kevin's dark eyes rolled. "*Yes,* for the third time." His shoulder jerked, and he stretched his neck irritably. "You should have brought Saul. I could have taken him with me, and then you could have flown off with Maalik."

I bristled at the accusation in his tone. "I'm not back with Maalik, Kevin."

He snorted and stuffed his hand down into the pockets of his robe. "Whatever. I don't care who you fu—"

"Enough." I stopped and turned to stand in his path, forcing him to look at me. "I'm your mentor, not your whipping post. I know you're hurting, but I am too, so cut it out." I hated to pull the boss lady card on him, but he'd brought it on himself.

Kevin's mouth snapped shut, and his jaw flexed. Tears tinted his eyes red, and he tilted his head up as if trying to keep them from spilling. His throat bobbed as he swallowed.

Though he didn't say anything more, I had the feeling that we were now locked in a staring contest, which I found annoying and ridiculous. Luckily, a gurney creaked behind Kevin, drawing his attention away for a split second.

"That's the last of them," I said, spinning around before he could resume the standoff. "I'll gather up the souls on this end. You go grab the ones in the morgue. We'll meet at the nurses' station." I stalked off down the hallway, not giving him a chance to argue.

The smell of charred flesh tickled my nose as I ducked past a nurse and through a pair of swinging doors. On the Posy Unit, fire victims were almost a daily staple of the job. I was just glad that today's lot was scheduled for pick-up at a hospital rather than the scene of the fire, which was more often the case. Of course, it was those miserable harvests, like the circus fire, where I actually needed Kevin. So, it would figure that he'd show up just in time for a cakewalk job.

The trauma center at the hospital was crowded. Most of the patients in the curtained-off rooms were from the fire, but I did have a gunshot wound on my list. A same time, same place happenstance.

Doctors and nurses bustled around, slinging the curtains open and closed as they went, creating a high-pitched symphony of metal on metal mixed with the hiss of fabric and the squeak of gurney wheels. I stood off in a corner until the room thinned out and quieted to the low hush of dying breaths.

The first body I came across was so crispy that I had to read the name across his chart in order to mark him off my list. He was a middle-aged guy named Ted, destined for Heaven. His brother was on my list, too, since they shared a room at the hotel, although he was sea-bound. Because my day didn't suck enough, apparently.

I'd just harvested my eighth soul, the gunshot victim, and was headed back to the nurses' station when I heard a woman scream bloody murder.

"Stay put," I said to my small herd of souls, waving my hand at them before taking off down the hall.

I dodged around a doctor as he backed out of a doorway and almost tripped over an abandoned wheelchair. My boots skidded across the linoleum as I rounded the corner, right before noticing the wet floor sign. I slipped and flopped against the far wall like a dead fish, the air in my lungs rushing out with an *oomph!*

At the end of the hall, the morgue doors were splayed wide open. Bloody fingers clung to the upper frame like someone was trying to peel themselves off the ceiling just inside. The scream came again, and then Kevin dropped to the floor.

For a moment, all I could do was gape. That sound had come from my apprentice. When a scaly, nude demon fell on his back, I understood why.

I scrambled down the hall, forgetting the slippery floor, and launched myself inside the room. As I tumbled gracelessly into the mayhem, I managed to grab hold of the demon's shoulders and pulled her off Kevin.

I hadn't planned the maneuver well, so it was little surprise that I ended up on the bottom when we landed.

"*Glack!*" I sputtered as her fingers squeezed around my throat.

She lifted her other hand, closing her fingers into a fist, and that's when I noticed her missing pinky. The world went slo-mo as my eyes shifted to her face. It was distorted with animalistic rage, but I saw her. Beelzebub's succubus.

I stopped trying to fend off her strangling hold and delivered a palm strike to her solar plexus. She hunched forward with a grunt, but her fist still connected with my temple.

Dark spots splattered across my vision as I rammed my palm into her sternum a second, and then a third time. She released my throat, scraping nails across my skin as she reached up to shield herself from my fourth strike. I could breathe again.

The room grew brighter as I sucked in a noisy breath. I yanked the demon's right arm and arched my left hip at the same time, toppling her over and off me. Her skull made a satisfying crack as it collided with the floor. I grabbed a handful of her tangled, black hair and lifted her head to slam it down again, grinning when it bounced, and she let out a garbled scream.

I was ready to give the nifty trick another go when her scaly foot swung around and nailed me in the ribs. I writhed on the floor and scooted away from her, squealing as she slithered after me. My back hit a wall, and I curled into myself, lifting my hands in front of my face. A loud clatter drew both of our attentions away.

Kevin held a metal tray with both hands. He shrieked and raised it over his head, bringing it down in a wide, sweeping arch. It hit the succubus in the face so hard that she rose from the floor and flopped onto her back. Blood gushed from her nose and mouth, spraying over the floor as she hissed at Kevin. He lifted the tray again, but she quickly fumbled a coin out of the pouch at her hip and disappeared.

CHAPTER SEVENTEEN

"Anger is never without a reason,
but seldom with a good one."
—Benjamin Franklin

"I fucking hate you." Kevin lay across one of the pristine, white couches in the condo with a bag of frozen peas pressed to the side of his face. "I'm serious," he said flatly as if the lack of energy behind his words might have somehow convinced me that they were insincere.

We'd managed to deliver the hospital souls to their afterlives, but I'd given our other two harvests to Kate and Alex. Kevin and I were both too rattled to deal with much more today.

I sat on the opposite couch, a bag of frozen corn tucked under my chin and around my neck. "It was just one demon. Don't be such a baby," I croaked. Then I glanced down at his bloody hand oozing onto the couch and added, "Holly's gonna skin you alive if she sees that."

His sunken eyes narrowed at me as he closed his hand into a fist and ground it into the cushion. "If I keep working for you, I doubt I'll have to worry about that much longer."

I heaved one of the frilly pillows across the room, hitting him square in the face. "Lots of reapers have been reporting demon attacks on the job lately. Read a paper, asshole."

Kevin threw the pillow aside with a growl and lifted his palm at me. "*Sanctus Incendia!*"

I rasped in disbelief and tossed the bag of corn in front of me to block the Latin incantation. The stream of fire that shot across the room ripped through the plastic, and soggy kernels rained down as I hurled myself over the coffee table at Kevin.

His eyes bulged, and the couch rocked backward, taking us with it. I couldn't tell if he was more surprised by his actions or mine. When my elbow pressed into the hollow of his throat, he gagged out a mangled protest.

"What was that?" I shouted in his face.

"Glah! I'm sorry," he wheezed, slapping at my arm as his eyes watered. His face turned red, then purple. Just when it seemed as though he might pass out, I eased off and stood.

The bag of frozen peas had burst open during our tussle, too. They were everywhere, along with the corn, stinking up the condo as they thawed. Saul crept into the living room, drawn by our noise, and sniffed at the skunky bits lodged in the rug.

Kevin rolled onto his side and panted, trying to catch his breath. "I'm sorry," he rasped again and choked out a sob.

Heat blossomed in my chest, and my skin itched. My hands were clenched so tightly that my nails cut into my palms. I had to get out of the condo. I couldn't be around Kevin right now.

"Clean up your mess and take a shower." I snatched my jacket out of the coat closet.

Kevin's breathing picked up speed as if he were getting ready to hyperventilate, and he began sobbing in earnest.

"Then eat something. The fridge is full," I snapped.

He didn't say anything, and I was out of stupid commands. I stormed out of the condo and slammed the front door behind me.

I'd just kicked Kevin's ass and, somehow, I still felt like a coward. He was clearly on the verge of falling apart, but I was so furious that I couldn't scrounge up enough sympathy to trust myself not to pull him out of existence. So, I'd run.

I didn't have anywhere in particular to go, which was usually the best time to hit up Purgatory Lounge, but not even the prospect of booze could cheer me up this time.

"Hey!" Warren hollered from the end of the hall as I stepped into an elevator. His flannel-clad arms waved furiously from the threshold of his condo. I reached my hand out as the elevator doors tried to slide shut.

The perky nephilim bounced down the hallway with a spear over each arm. He took a moment to assess the size of the elevator car and then tilted the weapons in diagonally.

"Gotta be careful with these beauties," he said with a grin. "The elevators are smaller here than at Reapers Inc. I learned that one the hard way." He cringed and blushed sheepishly.

"I see." I gave him a tight smile.

"You're off work early," he noted, giving me a curious frown. "And it appears your neck is quite swollen."

"Rough day on the job." I shrugged and tucked my hands into the pockets of my jacket.

"After I drop off these spears to the Guard, I'll be free for the evening if you'd like to give the bike a spin," he said hopefully.

It definitely sounded like a more useful way to spend my night. Besides, coming home drunk was probably not the best idea if Kevin decided to wait up for me. I needed my head clear if I was going to play Dr. Phil with him later.

I nodded at Warren. "Sure. I'll meet you in the garage in ten."

His wings gave an excited little flutter, and he nearly dropped the spears. "Oh, goody! I can't wait to see the bike in action."

We parted ways in the lobby, and I headed over to the small café just outside the gym to grab a bottle of water. The coffee smelled amazing, a dark foreign roast, but my nerves were still too raw to add caffeine to the mix.

Charlie, the ever-cheerful nephilim who ran the front desk of Holly House, whistled as he dusted the granite countertop facing the entrance. His meaty bear hands looked twice as large with a feather duster pinched between his thumb and forefinger. I knew Holly had likely hired him because of his intimidating size, but over the past few months, I'd come to realize that Charlie was an oversized puppy. I couldn't even look at him wrong without his wings going all droopy, and his bottom lip spilling out in a disgraced pout.

"Hiya, Charlie," I said as I passed his desk on my way to the garage exit.

He stopped whistling and stood straighter, fluffing his wings as he cleared his throat. "Good afternoon, Captain Harvey. Is there anything I can do for you?" He gave me a timid smile, and I noticed his chest rise as he took a measured breath.

My shitty mood and shotgun temper hadn't made me very popular lately. The eggshell treatment that seemed to follow my outbursts wasn't helpful either.

I pressed my lips together and shook my head. "I'm good, Charlie. Thanks."

In the reflection of the front window, I watched Charlie's shoulders sag with relief as I reached the door to the parking garage. My misery was infectious, and I'd somehow become a total wretch. How could I have let things get this bad?

I sighed and exited the lobby. When the door closed behind me, the garage was dark. Too dark. My boots crunched, and I glanced down to find glass sprinkled across the concrete. Someone had broken the light above the door, along with the lights spanning down the inside wall.

"Warren?" My voice echoed back to me in the darkness, and then it grew louder, shifting tone and texture until it felt like someone was standing right beside me. I gasped and took a step back, reaching for the door, but a shadowy figure stood in my path.

CHAPTER EIGHTEEN

My vision blurred, and the back of my head throbbed where it had thumped on the concrete floor of the garage. I blinked a few times and squinted up at the creatures crouched over me. *Creature*, I realized as the dancing outlines merged into one.

Fishy breath caressed my face as it leaned in closer, and I suppressed a gag, though that was mostly because I didn't want to choke on my own vomit. My assailant had a bony hand pressed firmly over my mouth. Her other hand was locked around one of my wrists, twisting my arm out to the side.

"They took him from me," she hissed. "Because of you!"

My eyes finally focused in the dim light, and I looked up into the face of the succubus for the second time in less than three hours. What the hell did a girl have to do to catch a break around here?

I grunted through her fingers and used my free hand to push her face away. She stumbled back on her heels before falling on her ass with a yelp.

"Ugh. Did you have roadkill for lunch, or what?" I waved a hand in front of my face as I stood and backed away, farther into the garage since the succubus was blocking the door.

She pulled herself up off the floor and pointed at me. "You will pay for this transgression. He was mine!"

I tapped a finger to my lips and grinned. "Oh, I see. Wow. The Lord of the Flies kicked you to the curb already?" I giggled and waved my hand at her. "That's too bad. You seem like such a catch. Or maybe you just smell like one."

Her face twisted up like a piece of overstretched taffy as her mouth opened, revealing two rows of teeth. Her scream shook the building. Someone surely heard. The Guard would be here any second. I was certain of it.

The succubus reached up and tore at her hair, coming away with greasy, tangled handfuls. She lowered her hands, uncurling her fingers and letting the hair settle at her feet. Her breath was ragged, and she had to swallow a few times before finding her voice again. "They will kill him if you do not bring the soul. He is mine, but only you can save him now."

A brigade of footsteps sounded at the other end of the garage, where it opened to the circle drive out front. The Guard was on their way. The succubus heard them, too. She fished a coin out of her hip pouch. It was a lumpy, red piece. Definitely not standard Eternity currency. She gave me a parting glare and rolled it, leaving me to wait alone in the dark.

If I hadn't been certain before, I was now. The rebels' prisoner was Bub. They were using him to manipulate me into handing over the throne soul, and they didn't care if Bub was actually a spy or not. The succubus clearly didn't think he was—or at least, she didn't seem to care.

My heart burned like charcoal with each beat, and as the Guard came into sight, a feeling of dread pooled in my stomach. What was I supposed to tell them?

The messenger soul's summoner ring was one thing, but if this little incident got back to Grim, he would definitely pay Winston a visit. He would demand an explanation for the faulty travel restrictions, and I could only imagine how well Winston would handle that conversation, especially if Grim went all inky-eyed on him.

There was only one thing I could do. I swallowed my pride and turned to face the feathered stampede, prepared to lie my ass off.

CHAPTER NINETEEN

'Friendship is always a sweet responsibility,
never an opportunity."
—Khalil Gibran

"Rats?" Jenni stared at me in disbelief. "At Holly House?" She shook her head and shuddered. "Holly is not going to be happy about this."

"Holly? How do you think *I* feel?" I hooked my feet around the bottom rung of the barstool and took a long swallow from my Ambrosia Ale.

The guards had not been thrilled when I insisted that the scream had been mine and that it was the result of rodents. I was beyond mortified that that was the best I could come up with on the spot, but better mortified than crucified. How's that for words to live by?

Warren had arrived just in time to vouch for why I was in the garage in the first place since the Guard was still having a hard time buying the rat ruse. I wanted to bail after they finally left us alone, but Warren was so excited, and I felt like I owed him for being the only nephilim who didn't look at me like a whack job when I mentioned the rats in the garage.

"That explains a lot," he had said breathlessly, glaring into the dark corners of the space. It was all the guards needed since my two-page statement didn't seem to be enough.

I spent an hour straddling the bike and tiptoeing it around his shop, but when Warren finally convinced me to fire it up, I found myself pinned between it and the concrete in two seconds flat. Warren was more concerned about a scuff in the bike's paint job than my busted ass, so it seemed like a good time to call it a night.

Jenni cleared her throat, and I realized I had missed something she said. "Any more thoughts on the soul's message or who their prisoner might be?" she repeated.

I felt my face flush. "No." I slid gingerly off the barstool and limped over to the fridge to grab another beer. "Kevin was actually at work today, and Gabriel called earlier to make sure we were still on for tomorrow night."

Jenni looked surprised. "Kevin showed up today?"

"And then the little shit took a cheap shot at me and almost set the condo on fire in the process."

She wriggled her nose. "I thought it smelled weird in here. I would have blamed it on Saul, but I couldn't find him."

"What?" I slammed the fridge door and set my beer on the counter before hobbling down the hall to Kevin's room. It didn't seem possible, but it looked even messier than before.

"Saul? Come here, boy." I patted my uninjured side, and when that didn't elicit a response, I moved on to my bedroom.

"I'm sure he's just with Kevin," Jenni shouted from the kitchen.

"That's what I'm afraid of." I checked my bathroom and closet just to be sure, but my apprentice and hellhound were nowhere to be seen. "Great. Just great." I limped back into the kitchen and snatched my beer off the counter.

Jenni shrugged. "How much trouble can he really get into if he has Saul with him?" I lowered my chin and gave her a cynical glare. "Stupid question. Forget I asked." She took a sip of her beer and picked up the remote, clicking on the big screen in the living room.

The evening news blared dismally through the condo. Reports of vandalism within the city and the skyrocketing number of CNH souls were nothing new, but a video clip of the creepy, ghost-eyed soul in front of Reapers Inc. caught my attention.

The demon anchorman looked shaken as if he were picturing himself being summoned against his will. He turned away from the footage and smiled uncomfortably at the camera. "The Nephilim Guard is offering a reward for anyone with information on the soul in question or the talisman used to assault the city."

His co-anchor, a perky nephilim in a fluorescent pink blouse and matching lip gloss, picked up where he left off. "More details to follow at the press conference tomorrow morning that we'll be covering live here on Channel Nine."

The news theme song faded off and was quickly replaced by a cheery waltz number as a commercial for Athena's Boutique flashed across the screen. Her wooden mannequins danced in a wide circle around the sales floor, past racks of sequined gowns and freshly pressed robes. A silky voice reminded viewers of the approaching ball and the super sale going on through Friday.

The next commercial was for a Sea of Eternity vacation cruise. Jenni clicked the television off before the announcer could jump in with the annoyingly familiar jingle, *"Ninety-nine, ninety-nine, is all it costs for one hell of a time!"* The cost had dropped significantly from last year's rate because no one wanted to vacation across a sea where a rebel ship could pop up any time they pleased.

Jenni and I sat in the kitchen for a while longer, side-by-side in quiet contemplation. The stretches of silence between us were usually more comfortable than this, but my thoughts bounced around more anxiously inside my skull tonight. I'd thought four days wasn't enough time, but now it felt like too much. My heart couldn't take much more.

After Jenni had headed off to bed, I decided to take a shower. A bath seemed too risky. With my current luck, I'd probably drown. When my aches were soothed, and the demon funk was washed down the drain, I curled up in bed by myself. I missed the hounds, even more on my vulnerable nights when sleep wasn't easy to come by.

I stared at the ceiling for half an hour before giving up and rummaging around in the top drawer of my nightstand for my tablet. I needed to check my email anyway. I hadn't been very consistent with the online crap lately, and Grace Adaline had given me hell for it more than once.

I answered a few students' homework questions, ignored one very nosy, baited *glad demons didn't eat your face off* message from a minor goddess, and then paused on an email from

Jack. He'd worked up a mock midterm test, scrambling the study guide questions we passed out the night before. He was the best, and I was determined to talk Grace into giving him the class next semester. Demon prejudice be damned.

If anyone deserved the truth about Bub, it was Jack. I had the urge to call him up and tell him everything, but I knew that was probably my loneliness talking more than anything else. Then I wondered if Bub had tried to contact Jack. Maybe that could account for the rebels finding out that he was a spy. Or perhaps he had tried to contact Cindy.

I hadn't seen Bub since our unplanned tryst right after the battle on the mortal seas, the one where we'd lost Josie. Bub had confessed his secret mission to me on the hidden ledge behind the ruins of his manor in Tartarus. *After* I'd thrown myself at him.

Even now, knowing that he was one of the good guys, I felt ashamed when I remembered that moment. I'd just lost my best friend, and I was still under the impression that Bub was on the side that had taken her from me. How could I even *think* about sex, let alone with him?

The burden of my guilt had lifted only slightly by his revelation, but my spirits dropped just as quickly when I realized he couldn't stay. He had to go back to the rebels, back to that succubus, and I might not ever see him again.

Was it wrong that a part of me was glad the rebels wanted to trade him back to us? Back to me? Of course, there was no way I could turn over Naledi, not even if I wanted to. You couldn't barter with something you didn't have. Plus, I had it on good authority that Armageddon was no carnival ride.

Still. There had to be something I could do.

I tossed and turned for another hour before finally drifting off into a fitful sleep, only to be consumed by nightmares of Bub and the succubus. Bub being tortured by rebels. Bub standing over me and laughing for falling for a rebel trick. Bub being the biggest rebel trick of all.

CHAPTER TWENTY

"We hang the petty thieves
and appoint the great ones to public office."
—Aesop

Wednesday was worthless. Kevin was off the grid again. Big surprise there. The harvest list was heavy and miserable, directing more souls into the sea and to Hell than I'd seen in a long time. Even Arden was vexed enough to vocalize his distaste for my leniency with Kevin.

At least he waited until we were off on a harvest together, away from the rest of the unit, before giving me what I suspected was the closest thing to a lecture he had ever delivered.

"Loss is never pleasant, least of all for our young, but it is up to us to teach them the appropriate ways and limits of grief," he said in his slow, smooth-as-butter voice as we climbed through the aftermath of a bombed military base.

"Our young?" I scoffed. "You make them sound like children."

"Yes." He stepped over a fallen steel beam and then reached back to lend me a hand. "They are exactly like children. These experiences are all new, and they need firm direction to navigate them."

I grumbled a noncommittal sound. He was right, of course. Arden didn't say much, but when he did, it was always worth listening to.

He considered me a moment longer, the whites of his eyes glowing softly in the shadow of the debris. "Saul Avelo was a fine reaper. You can trust his training to see you through this." He touched a finger to the side of his dark, shaved head. "I know it's still in there."

I felt my cheeks warm. "You seem to know plenty about mentoring. Why didn't you sign up for an apprentice last year?"

The corners of his mouth pulled up into a sad smile. "You've seen my ship. I know more than I care to about mentoring." He turned away, ending our brief conversation, and headed deeper into the wreckage.

I'd almost forgotten about Arden's previous position on the Mother Goose Unit. His sailing partner, Asha Dipika was still a member, and while the Posy Unit didn't focus on child souls, it wasn't uncommon for them to end up on our docket occasionally. Arden was usually the first to claim those harvests.

His and Asha's ship featured a carousel on the main deck. It was one of the oddest custom upgrades I'd ever seen, and it was even stranger to witness the two demure reapers taking turns operating the controls of the thing and passing out cotton candy. It almost reminded me of a scene from a cheesy, circus horror film Gabriel had once forced me to watch—after which I'd sworn my allegiance to John Wayne, forever and ever, amen.

Arden didn't say anything more during our harvest, and we soon parted ways. I had six more stops on my list, so it was dusk by the time I made it back to Holly House. Kevin wasn't home, and his cabin on the ship had been deserted, too.

I had nothing better to do with myself, and I couldn't see sitting around the empty condo with unanswered questions and worst-case-scenario fantasies playing through my head, so I joined Warren in the garage again.

The overhead lights had been replaced, and a handful of black, orbed security cameras lined the concrete walls. Warren had touched up the glossy paint on the bike, and he wrapped thin, rubber guards around the gas tank and fenders before letting me near it again. It was a good thing, too. After falling flat on my face a dozen times in the parking garage, I finally gave up and sulked off to lick my wounds.

Holly cornered me at the elevators. "Rats? You're sure?" She propped her dainty hands on her hips and grimaced as she looked me over. The flannel shirt I'd borrowed from Warren was torn in several places and speckled with grease and blood.

"Mm-hmm," I mumbled through the sleeve pressed up under my bloody nose. I reached around her and pushed the button for the elevator, earning another sour look.

"I just can't believe we didn't catch any of them with the traps we put out last night—or the new cameras I had installed." She shook her head and huffed out a skeptical breath.

"Perhaps her bloodcurdling scream scared them all off," Charlie offered from the front desk.

I lifted my eyebrows thoughtfully and squinted at my reflection in the elevator door. "It's possible," I said, fingering
the dried blood along the edge of one nostril. Holly looked
entirely disgusted. Mission accomplished. "When my hell-
hounds get home, I'll walk them around the garage to see if
they can locate a nest."

"Nest?" Holly choked out.

"Well, sure." An elevator pinged open, and I stepped inside. "Where there's one, there's many." I grinned at her
horrified expression and waved my bloody sleeve as the doors
closed.

When I stepped off the elevator, my boots left a smear of
grease on the beige carpet in the hallway. I swore and yanked
them off before padding past a gold-framed rendering of
cherubs playing poker on the way to my condo. My keys jingled as I unlocked the front door, and an excited yap sounded
on the other side. My heart stuttered.

I threw open the door and dropped to my knees, bracing
for the impact of Saul's greeting. He didn't disappoint. The
hound's paws found my shoulders and rocked me back, slam-
ming me into the carpet as his rough tongue lapped up the
side of my face, leaving a trail of drool along my hairline and
in my ear.

"There he is!" I laughed as relieved tears leaked from my
eyes. My fingers tangled in his dark fur, and I didn't even care
that he smelled as if he'd recently rolled in something dead.

Saul was an intimidating beast, but he was still a puppy at
heart. I should have been able to trust Kevin with his care,
but my apprentice's current condition had left me more

anxious than I wanted to admit. I knew he was more concerned with his habit than properly caring for my hound, and I was beyond pissed that he hadn't brought Saul home the night before.

"Come on, boy." I ruffled Saul's ears and sat up.

Gabriel and Jenni stood in the doorway, their arms folded and dark expressions on their faces. Neither of them said a word.

"Where's Kevin?" I asked, using Saul's shoulder to pull myself up off the floor.

They exchanged a sour look, coming to some silent agreement before backing up to clear a path into the condo for me.

"We don't know," Gabriel answered stiffly as he closed the front door behind me. "Saul was found over on Westwood Road. The Nephilim Guard called me to come and collect him. They've been watching one of the apartments over there for rebels, but no one has confirmed any sighting of Kevin."

"Great." I opened the coat closet to put away my boots, wedging them in beside the giant bag of Cerberus Chow before refilling Saul's food bowl. His tail beat against my leg, wagging so hard that his hind end bobbed around in a happy little dance. When I placed the dish on the floor, he buried his muzzle in the kibble.

Jenni raised an eyebrow. "That's his third bowl tonight."

If Kevin ever did come back, I was going to wring his scrawny little neck. It was one thing to completely disregard his own basic needs, but to be so careless with my poor furbaby was unforgivable.

"There's something else." Jenni cleared her throat and cast another worried look at Gabriel before turning back to me. "You might want to check your room. A few of my collectible swords are missing, and I have a feeling Kevin didn't stop there."

I took a deep breath, and then another. The tingle of my wrath was bubbling under my skin, and tonight was becoming complicated enough without having to explain the curious side effects of my rage.

I walked past Jenni and Gabriel and down the hall. My door was cracked, and my breath grew tighter as I pushed it open. The bed was unmade like I'd left it, but both of my nightstand drawers had been pulled out and dumped across the crinkled bedspread. I could tell from the remains that my tablet and a stash of coin I kept for pizza delivery was missing. *Bastard.*

My closet light was on, too. A few dresses had been knocked from their hangers, and several boxes were piled carelessly on the floor, their lids scattered in front of the shoes lined up against the inside wall. My breath caught as I knelt down to finger through ripped tissue paper, and tears blurred my vision.

The crystal bands Saul had given me when my apprenticeship ended were gone. The tablet could be replaced, and so could the coin, but the crystal bands had been a token of a hundred years spent under the wing of the best reaper—the best man—I'd ever known.

To have my own apprentice rob me of them felt like cruel karma, and it made my heart even heavier. Maybe I deserved this. Maybe Kevin's condition *was* my fault.

I sniffed and rubbed my sleeve under my nose, coming away with snot and blood. Everything hurt, inside and out, and I was far too tired to keep my resolve tonight.

A warm hand squeezed my shoulder. "Hey," Gabriel said, kneeling down behind me. His wings twitched as he took in the carnage and my tear-streaked face.

"Little shit cleaned me out." I tried to laugh, but it came out as a choked sob instead.

Gabriel swallowed and gave me a strained smile. "We'll get this all sorted out soon enough. Why don't you change into something more comfortable? I think we deserve a little break, and I have just the thing."

I sniffled again and nodded, not trusting my voice. At least Kevin had left my cupcake pajamas and fuzzy slippers alone. They were splayed across the bed, having been dumped from the bottom drawer of my nightstand.

I waited for Gabriel to leave before changing and then paused in my bathroom to more thoroughly clean the grease and blood from my face. The circles under my eyes were dark and angry. I looked old. Tired. When had that happened?

I walked back down the hallway in a daze, feeling numb and disconnected. Nothing seemed real. Was this what my life had become without Josie around to micromanage?

A dozen black frames hung along the stretches of wall between the condo's three bedrooms. They had been Josie's idea. I paused on a picture of the two of us standing in front of the ship the day we purchased it. Next to it was a snapshot she'd taken of Kevin while he worked on one of the new cabins. There was another of me, Josie, and Gabriel, sitting in a booth at Purgatory Lounge several years back before everything had veered off course. I looked so happy. So clueless.

Farther down the wall, there was a picture of Jenni in the old apartment she had shared with Josie before they moved in with me. She sat on a wide windowsill, her nose tucked in a book. The light spilling through the window was almost celestial, and Josie had developed the picture in black and white to best capture it.

I scanned the wall again, looking for any more that might have Josie in them, but there was just the two. There were probably more in her bedroom. In *Kevin's* bedroom. It was so hard to make the distinction, and the thought tightened my gut as I wondered if Kevin had pillaged through her effects too, to see what he could cash in for drugs.

I didn't know how just yet, but as soon as he surfaced, I was going to make things right. I couldn't give him a free pass for his grief, but I could make sure he got the help he needed. Arden was right. This was my responsibility. I had to be strong. Tough as coffin nails.

John Wayne called from the living room. Big Jake. It was one I knew by heart. He was getting ready to save the sheep farmer and his son. It seemed like a pretty compassionate move for someone who was estranged from his own sons. I guess the audience needed some indication that he was the good guy. I shuffled on down the hall as I heard the crinkle and pop of a snack bag.

Jenni swore. "Really? Don't you think these couches have seen enough abuse?"

I rounded the corner and saw Gabriel cram a handful of Cheetos into his mouth before grumbling crunchily at her. Jenni curled her nose at him and lifted an ice bucket stuffed with Ambrosia Ale off the coffee table to reveal a puddle underneath. She fumed as she mopped it up with a checkered dish towel. I thought she was going to come unhinged when I sat down on the opposite couch and Saul jumped up next to me.

"He needs a bath," she snapped.

I shrugged. "Saint Rocco's Doghouse closed last week."

"Then dunk him in Kevin's tub. It's not like he's using it."

Gabriel snorted. "That's sure to put a feather up Holly's ass." He propped his feet up on the table, and Jenni instantly shoved them off.

"Smells like you need a bath, too," Jenni said, leaning away from him as he made a mocking face, silently mouthing off with a puppet hand pointed in her direction. Cheesy crumbs peppered the couch between them.

"That's it!" she squealed. "Give me those."

Gabriel held away the bag of Cheetos as she crawled over his lap, reaching for them. He laughed and poked at her ribs, earning another frustrated squeal.

I couldn't help but giggle. "Come on, Josie—" I bit my tongue as they froze and turned toward me. "I'm sorry. I didn't mean—it just slipped out. I'm so sorry, Jenni."

She pulled away from Gabriel and smoothed her hands down her stomach, her eyes focused on the floor. "It's okay."

Gabriel's brows drew up and together. He gave me a soft smile and nodded to the television. "Here comes the good part."

We all looked up to watch Big Jake's reunion with his bitter son, where he gets bent out of shape over being called "Daddy."

Jenni looked confused. "He'd really rather be called a son of a bitch?"

Gabriel pointed an orange finger at her. "Don't try to understand the nature of the Duke all in one sitting, pilgrim."

I nodded in agreement. "It's an acquired flavor of nonsense."

Jenni finally managed to steal the Cheetos bag from Gabriel and carefully extracted a morsel with her thumb and forefinger, cringing when her knuckles brushed the edge of the bag and came away dusted orange. "This is impossible."

Gabriel took the bag back. "It's a proven fact that the tastiness of a snack is proportional to its messiness. It's a snacky conundrum." Jenni rolled her eyes at him. "Says so right in the Bible," he added, earning an eye roll from me, too.

I didn't say much the rest of the night, too afraid to break the *normal* spell. Saul stayed curled up at my side. His smelly, warm fur was reassuring, and I ended up nodding off a time or two during the remainder of the film. I woke up about the time the bad guys found out that they'd been duped. I liked it when bad guys got duped.

Gabriel was snoring loudly on the opposite couch, his head rolled back over the armrest, blond curls bobbing in time with each breath. I smiled as I watched him. I was really going to miss our movie dates if the world ended Saturday.

Jenni was missing from the other side of the couch, probably tucked away in her quiet bed. I was used to the chainsaw background noise, thanks to the hounds. Speaking of, Saul's droopy jowls were laid across my lap, a fine layer of slobber soaking through my pajama pants. He grumbled in his sleep when I reached for the remote to turn off the television.

As I lay back on the couch, I looked up at the ceiling and wondered where Bub was right this moment. Was he in pain? Was he afraid? Wondering if I would come for him?

Part of me felt as if I should be doing something more, maybe crusading through the afterlives, looking for him. Looking for Naledi. Looking for a rebel base to firebomb. I felt entirely helpless, but attempting to do anything worthwhile was sure to put me on Grim's radar.

I was down to three days. Three days before the boss man came for my head. And only two before someone relieved Bub of his. Weren't we a fine pair?

CHAPTER TWENTY·ONE

"A man can fail many times, but he isn't a failure until he begins to blame somebody else."
—John Burroughs

Thursday morning, the thumping of Saul's tail in my face woke me. I didn't piss and moan over it too much after I realized that I had slept through my alarm. All work and no play was starting to take its toll.

My skin crawled when I stepped outside Holly House. I could feel eyes watching me again. Saul sensed my discomfort and tilted his muzzle from side to side to sniff the air. He let out a gruff snort, seemingly frustrated that he couldn't zero in on the cause of my distress. We hurried past the front gate and to the travel booth across the street.

I was in and out of Reapers Inc. as if the place were on fire. Bumping into Grim was at the far, red end of my stress-o-meter, right before being eaten alive by hellcats. Which didn't seem as likely to happen, but I'd witnessed it enough times that I couldn't dismiss it entirely.

The harvest list Ellen gave me was deceptively light. I would have taken the time to question her about it, but like I said, raging red stress-o-meter to fret over. There were no protests from the Posy Unit, even though Kevin was still

MIA. Having Saul back helped the day slip by faster, and if not for the threat of Armageddon and the thought of Bub as a prisoner of war, I might have actually had a skip in my step.

I found myself back at Reapers Inc. by early afternoon. With Grim on the verge of smiting me, I probably shouldn't have, but I went ahead and risked bringing Saul into the office. I lucked out and missed the grimmest of reapers, but still somehow managed to run into Maalik in the lobby.

"Stalker alert," I quipped dryly. "You're totally following me, aren't you?"

Maalik gave me a forced smile as Saul nudged his leg for attention. It had been several months since we split, but the hounds still adored him. Especially Saul. The dirty little traitor. I was never bringing him to the office again.

"We need to talk," Maalik said, following me outside. Saul's tongue flopped out of his mouth as he happily pranced between us to keep up. Every time I saw the angel of doom and gloom, my stride seemed to double in length.

"I'm off work early. Don't spoil it." I groaned as Maalik grabbed my arm and steered me in the opposite direction of the nearest travel booth.

"Somewhere private. How about the park?"

"What? No. I'm going home to take a bath." I jerked my arm, but Maalik hung on. "I gave you the stupid tracker. You didn't think I was capable. Now, it's your problem. I gave up, remember? You win. Ow!"

"Quit being so difficult," he hissed, his fingers pinching around my elbow.

"Then quit manhandling me!"

A nephilim gave us a strange look and sidestepped around us as we stopped at the curb. Maalik mean-mugged him as he hurried away. A cab sputtered by, and then we were alone again. Limbo's afternoons had always been quiet, but today the city felt like a ghost town.

I glared at Maalik and finally jerked my arm free. "I don't understand why you can't just leave me alone. What more do you want from me?" I asked, straightening the sleeve of my jean jacket.

He cast a shifty look down the sidewalk and across the street, and then he stepped in closer to me, his dark hair almost curtaining our faces. "Have the rebels tried to contact you again?"

"No." I felt my pulse push at my temple, and I was sure the vein there was ratting me out in Morse code. The succubus hadn't actually contacted me on behalf of the rebels. So it didn't count, right?

Maalik narrowed his eyes and tilted his head as if he thought he could stare me into a confession. Then he sighed and shoved his hand down into the pocket of his robe, retrieving the tracking compact. "I need you to show me how this thing works."

My eyes widened in outrage. "I told you to read a fucking book."

"I did. Several," he muttered. "I followed the diagrams precisely, but to no avail. Are you sure you didn't break it?"

"Me?" I poked a finger in his chest. "I brought back two souls with it. If anyone broke the damn thing, it's you."

Maalik lifted his free hand and waved it in a down-girl motion. "Now, now. Throwing blame around isn't going to do us any good."

"*You* started it," I snapped, not caring how childish I sounded. I went ahead and stuck out my tongue to further prove it. "And *us*? There is no *us*. Got it? If the world ends Saturday, it's on you."

I paused to take a deep, rasping breath. My lungs just couldn't get enough air, and Maalik was inching back like I was the big, bad wolf trying to blow him down. My skin was on fire, and a sickly, familiar sensation radiated through me. Saul whimpered, and his ears fell flat against his head.

There was something in the way Maalik looked at me that said he knew more than he was ready to admit. Not just about the rebels or Naledi's whereabouts, but about me. He could tell I was on the verge of imploding.

"I'm asking for your help," he said evenly, placing his hand over his heart.

"You blackmailed me into giving you that thing, and now you can eat it for all I care." I swallowed and tried to slow my frantic breath.

Saul lifted his muzzle and ran it along my knuckles, darting his tongue out to lick my fingertips. He moved farther away from Maalik and pressed his shoulder against my knee, letting me know that he was on my side, no matter what.

Maalik gave him a nervous frown before looking back to me. "I'm sorry. You're right. I shouldn't have dismissed you so harshly, and I understand your resentment. But if the world ends Saturday, you end with it. Please, help me." He grabbed my hand and pressed the compact into my palm. "Please."

My shoulders slumped, and I groaned. How was I supposed to refuse Maalik after something that heartfelt? I could be angry again after Saturday. If we were still here, that is.

As I twisted the lid of the compact and folded it back on itself, Maalik leaned over to watch. His eyes swelled intently as if he had done this a million times, but he was sure there was some trick I knew that he was missing. His hair dangled in the way, and I had to nudge his shoulder back before continuing.

"There's really not that much to it," I said, twisting the folded top piece around to lie flat on the base. Nothing happened. I handed it back to Maalik and shrugged. "I don't know what's wrong with it. The last time it went off for me, I didn't even do anything."

"Well, try again," he insisted, holding the device out to me.

I opened my hands and backed away. "I'm sorry. That's the best I've got. Maybe it can't detect Naledi if she's on the mortal side. The rebels have been known to hide out over there."

Of course, that was complete bullshit. The bracelets were designed to work just fine on both sides, but I had a feeling if Maalik knew that, he'd keep badgering me until I took a hammer to the device.

He looked thoughtful. "Do you suppose that's why Grim's captive was able to summon demons? Because the throne soul's absence has left Eternity vulnerable?"

The succubus and her lumpy red coin came to mind again, and I cringed. "Sure. I'll buy that."

"But it doesn't explain why the rebels are still requesting a worthy soul." His eyes darkened skeptically again. "You don't happen to know where a peak marked in fool's blood is, do you? It seems to be the only piece of the puzzle no one has surmised, and since the message was directed at you, I have to wonder…" He trailed off.

"Sorry." I stuffed my hands into the pockets of my jacket. "Guess I'm completely useless today. Good luck with saving the world, though." I stepped around him, only to have my arm snatched again.

Maalik leaned his head over my shoulder, forcing my eyes to meet his. The deep brown was swirled through with smoke, a faint reminder of the hellfire within. "I still care for you, Lana. But so help me, if you're withholding vital information so you can rescue that traitorous fiend, I will seek you out with a vengeance."

My chest tightened as I lifted my chin. "You asked for my help, and I gave it. I believe the appropriate response is 'thank you.' Or has a year in politics already corrupted your manners so severely?" I held his hateful gaze until he let go.

"Don't be a fool, Lana," he said under his breath, then turned and stalked away.

"You're welcome!" I shouted after him, just for spite.

I might have been a fool, but I was an idiot with a plan. And thanks to Maalik, I now knew exactly where the rebels would be waiting for me Friday night.

CHAPTER TWENTY·TWO

*"Be kind, for everyone you meet
is fighting a hard battle."*
—*Philo*

Maalik was still following me. I couldn't see him, but I knew he was there, lurking in the shadows. I'd felt it all week. It was as if he thought I was going to rush off to some lair where I had Naledi tied up for a rainy day of sabotage. I only half wished that was true.

If it came right down to it, I didn't think I could actually turn her over to the rebels and bring about the end of all things. But watching Big Jake's Kansas City Shuffle last night had helped stir up a sneaky idea on how to get around that. I just needed to ditch Maalik.

I couldn't risk going back to the throne realm this early in the day. It was too likely that Maalik—or Khadija help me, Grim—would pop in at the wrong time, and then the bad idea I was brewing would be useless. I had to find something non-incriminating to occupy myself with until nightfall. Otherwise, I would end up chewing my fingernails down to the cuticles in my restless paranoia.

The bike had been a good distraction so far. I spent a few more hours working with Warren again, doing laps around the parking garage, and left feeling like less of a failure than I had in a long time. I didn't fall on my face once, and Warren actually took the rubber bumpers off to show how impressed he was with my progress.

We made plans to take the bike out on the streets of Limbo the following week after the ball traffic had dissipated, because I didn't have the heart to tell him we probably wouldn't see past Saturday. My panic had to remain private if I didn't want to forfeit the few days I had left.

I also had to rein in any optimism in order to keep Maalik at bay. It was a tricky balance, and the fear that I wasn't pulling it off seemed to worsen my condition. There was a twinge in my chest as if my blood pressure had capped off, and my heart beat out an error message: *Get your shit together.*

I made my way upstairs and entered the condo to the smell of fresh Thai food. A row of open boxes lined the breakfast bar, and Jenni was digging through the kitchen drawers. "Do we have any chopsticks around here?" she asked.

"Left of the sink, second down," I said, ogling the savory spread. "Where did you get this? I thought the Thai place in Limbo shut down."

"They did," Jenni answered, digging around in the drawer I'd directed her to until she found a couple sets of sticks. She passed a pair to me. "But their location inside the gates of Nirvana is still doing quite well."

I let out a little squeal of joy and nearly welled up. "This is perfect." *For a last meal,* I silently added.

Jenni blinked at me. "Wow, you really love your Thai food."

I grinned and tapped my chopsticks to hers before digging in.

It occurred to me as we ate, that although I was still scheming to put together a rescue mission for Bub, I had accepted that the world could actually end Saturday. Naledi was either dead, a captive of an unknown entity, or she didn't want to be found. None of which did me any good. All of which would result in the onset of Armageddon if not resolved by Saturday.

I wanted to visit the few people I cared about, just to tell them how much they meant to me, but again, that would open the door for questions I couldn't answer. I imagined Maalik was struggling through his own set of doomsday emotions. I wanted to feel sorry for him, but his accusations hurt. We should have been exchanging kinder words, maybe apologizing for the past.

The only thing keeping me from sinking into depression was the fantasy of being reunited with Bub.

"You're quiet tonight." Jenni interrupted my thoughts as she slurped a spoonful of soup.

I folded my arms over the bar. "Just thinking."

"About what?"

"This, that, and the other."

She opened her mouth and paused as if she wanted to say something more but couldn't bring herself to. It was a painful look, the kind that suggested she was struggling with being a good friend and being a good minion.

"No," I said flatly. "I still don't know the meaning of that soul's message."

I had a feeling Grim hadn't actually put her up to asking me. He wouldn't want her to know about Winston or the throne realm. Jenni was just being Jenni, doing her job well. I hated lying to her, but there was no other way.

"How's the interrogation going?" I asked, trying to sound like I cared whether or not Grim solved the riddle.

Jenni cringed away from the question. Her face paled as she cleared her throat. "Well, Grim retrieved the ring she was using to summon demons with."

"And by retrieved, do you mean he dug through her excrement, or removed it from her intestinal track with a pair of pliers?"

"Does it matter?" She shuddered and dropped her chopsticks to the counter. "Turns out, it's the Seal of Solomon. It was thought lost for some time. We don't know how long it's been in the soul's possession."

"So that's how she managed to summon the demons." It made sense. Solomon had used the ring to enslave demons to build his temple. Now, the soul was using it to vandalize the city. Kids today just had no imagination.

Jenni nodded slowly. "She hasn't given us anything else."

"Grim losing his edge? And by edge, I mean do his interrogation tools need a whetstone?" I gave her a callous look.

Jenni pressed her lips together and turned away, swallowing hard and breathing in through her nose. "She smiles at me. Every time I come into the room. I don't know how she does it. I remember being tortured by the rebels, but what Grim's doing to her…” Her hands began to tremble, and she quickly clasped them, tucking them under the counter and out of view. “Killing her would be a mercy at this point.”

“I’m sorry,” I said, feeling like a shit for bringing up unpleasant memories. “Once the ball is over, I’m sure Grim will feel less inclined to pump her for information.” I kept the bit about how an apocalypse would totally take care of that to myself.

Jenni nodded and pushed her dinner away before propping her elbows on the counter. “I find my ambition wavering these days. I’m at the top of the food chain. This is what all reapers aspire to—”

“*Most.*” I cleared my throat.

She snorted. “—*most* reapers aspire to. I just wish I could take a step back. This isn’t what I signed up for.”

I reached across the counter and squeezed her arm. “You’re the best reaper for the job, and you know it. As much as I hate Grim, I think he honestly believes he’s in the right, and I try to believe it myself most days.”

“Me, too.” Jenni laughed. “He doesn’t make it easy, though.”

The doorbell rang, and we both jumped at the churchy tune. I gave Jenni a sheepish grin and slid off my barstool to answer the door.

Ross stood in the hallway. A lumpy sack of bones that took me a minute to recognize as my apprentice stood before him.

CHAPTER TWENTY-THREE

"Colleagues are a wonderful thing—but mentors,
That's where the real work gets done."
—Junot Diaz

My mouth fell open. Kevin's head had been shaved. His thin arms hung limply at his sides, and there were fresh track marks in the bends of his elbows. He wasn't wearing shoes, and his toenails were dark and cracked.

Ross's wings gave a quick flap behind him, and Kevin jolted into awareness, turning his dull eyes up to me.

"I'm not a babysitter, Lana." Ross looked less than thrilled to be having this conversation with me. His brows sank into a warning line. "If he screws up a third time, I'm taking him to Grim."

"I'm not sure he'd survive another screw-up. Look at him." I waved my hand in front of Kevin's face. His eyes had unfocused again, and I wasn't even certain he knew where he was.

Ross nudged him forward and into the condo. "Also, I found some receipts on him from the pawn shop over on Tombstone Drive. They've been known to deal with stolen goods, but we've been more focused on the hellfire dens and rebel bases on that side."

"Thanks. I'll check them out next week." Because I sure as hell wasn't going to waste my time haggling with a crook if I could get around it by dying Saturday. Who says Armageddon can't have a silver lining?

Ross gave me a curt salute and left without another word. I tugged Kevin inside and closed the front door, turning around in time to watch Jenni slap him across the face. It hardly seemed to register for him.

"I've had some of those swords for nearly five hundred years," she hissed. "Half a millennium! You're going to track down every last one of them and return them to me."

I wedged myself between her and Kevin, lifting my hands to fend her off. "He's not even coherent right now. Save the threats and lectures for when he's sober." Her eyes widened maliciously, and her nostrils flared. "I mean, unless you need the practice. But you think we could save it for after bath time? Because, oh my gods, he reeks."

Jenni folded her arms across her chest, digging her fingers into her biceps. "Fine."

I steered Kevin down the hall and into his room. I hadn't had the nerve to really take a good look in there after he robbed us, and now I was glad for it.

Josie's drawers had been dumped out onto the floor. I don't know why I was surprised that her things were still in the dresser. I knew Kevin had left several of her personal items around the room, and much of her clothing still hung in the closet. It just didn't occur to me that he wouldn't have at least cleared out a few of her things for the sake of moving on. Of course, that would have been rational, something he was clearly having trouble mastering.

A wooden jewelry box lay open on the bed. Except for a pair of hoop earrings, it was empty. The emerald necklace Apollo had given Josie to wear to the Oracle Ball last year was missing. It was hard telling what else.

I swallowed my anger and pushed Kevin into the bathroom. It was a nice setup, though more modest than mine. A giant, silver squid hung on the wall, its tentacles fashioned into towel hooks, and a shadowbox frame full of dried starfish hung above the toilet. A fluffy, white rug stretched out in front of the tub, enclosed by a pair of sliding glass doors.

"Strip." I pointed at the filthy tank top and jeans Kevin wore, hanging so loosely from him that I doubted they had ever fit. When he didn't move, I clapped my hands in front of his face. "Hey! Listen up, or I'll call Ross back and have him take you to Grim now. No one owes you a third chance."

He grunted something unintelligible but finally started moving around like a living thing and pulled the scrap of shirt over his head. I turned on the faucet in the shower and cranked the dial over to the coldest setting, which inspired real words once I shoved Kevin inside.

"Holy shit," he stammered, his shoulders hunching up around his ears. He tried to backpedal out of the shower, but I stood guard at the open door, holding my hand against the frame to keep the other glass panel from sliding open.

"Suck it up, champ," I said, tossing him a bar of soap. "You're not coming out of there until you've scrubbed every bit of that funk off. If you don't like the cold, then hurry it up. You can take a hot shower on your own time."

Kevin groaned in protest, but his hands worked faster, shivering as he lathered up his face and pits. He slowed a moment when he reached his bald head as if he hadn't noticed until now that his hair was missing. I turned away when he got to his man bits, giving him a few seconds of privacy.

"Don't forget your feet," I shouted through the door.

When he was finally done, I turned off the faucet and handed him a towel. He ran it over his face and chest before wrapping it around his waist and stepping out onto the rug. His eyes were more focused, but they still had an odd coloring to them, and his skin, though clean, looked ashen and patchy.

He blinked at me and then looked around the bathroom as if it were all foreign to him. "What now?" he asked.

"Now you get dressed, and we clean your room."

"Why?"

"Because I said so, that's why."

His chest puffed out defiantly, but the ribs and veins pressing through his skin killed the effect. "This is stupid."

"No, this is easy." I folded my arms. "Being turned over to Grim because you're too stubborn to follow the orders of your mentor would be stupid."

"Is that what it's come to?" His breath huffed out in disgust. "I can follow orders or get lost?"

"No. No getting lost. You've done enough of that lately."

Kevin ground his teeth and growled under his breath. He stomped back into the bedroom and grabbed a shirt off the floor, yanking it over his head hard enough that the fabric complained, threads popping along the seams. He pulled on a pair of gym shorts next before flopping down on the edge of the bed and folding his arms over his knees. He looked around the room, taking in the damage he had done, and his eyes watered.

I made a quick trip to the kitchen to grab a few trash bags. When I came back, Kevin was on the floor, holding one of Josie's sweaters to his chest. Tears poured soundlessly down his face. I shook open a bag and picked up a pair of Josie's socks that had been scattered during Kevin's drug-induced plundering.

"Wait!" He held his hand out. "What are you doing? Those are Josie's. You can't just throw them away."

"Are you going to wear them?"

"You can't throw them away," he repeated louder.

I sighed and bent down to pick up another pair. "Fine. But they're not staying here. We'll put them in the storage unit."

"But—" His eyes widened, and he began to pant as he snatched up an armful of Josie's clothes, holding them away from me. "No!"

I sat on the edge of the bed and ran a shaky hand over my face. "Look, Kevin. I know this is hard, but we're going to get through it together. Okay?" I waved my hand around the room. "This is no way to live."

He took a heaving breath and stifled a sob. Of all the things I'd said and done trying to get through to him, I hadn't expected this to sink his battleship.

"I need more time," he pleaded, his eyes begging me to have mercy.

"We're all out of time, grasshopper." Boy, didn't I know it.

I gave Kevin another minute to pull himself together and then held out the bag. He rubbed his face against the mound of fabric and then very gently nestled it inside the bag. His eyes welled, and I thought he might lose it again, but he didn't.

We spent the next hour bagging up every bit of Josie's clothes and shoes. Then we moved on to her personal things in the bathroom, including her girly shampoos. It wasn't like Kevin could use them right now anyway. He hesitated on a few items—her perfume and hand lotion—but coaxing him to let go did get easier. I caved at the bookshelf and left it alone for the most part. Kevin could actually use those, and the purpose of this little chore wasn't to erase Josie entirely but rather to give Kevin a fresh start.

When we finished, I set the bags by the front door. We dusted and vacuumed next, polishing the dresser and moving Kevin's clothing around to fill all the drawers, even if he only had enough for an item or two in each. The absence of Josie's knickknacks made the space feel a little empty, but it finally felt like a bedroom again instead of a poorly kept museum. I set Kevin to work washing his bedding and took a break to share a beer in the kitchen with Jenni.

She glanced at the bags lined up against the wall and then at Kevin as he passed through the living room with an empty hamper. "You think it will last?" she asked quietly.

"It's the best I can do right now. I'll talk to Meng after the ball."

I frowned at my beer as I thought about all the things I was pushing off until after Saturday. It really put my priorities into perspective, which reminded me of how much I missed Coreen. It had been a week since I called to check in on her and the pups at Apollo's temple in Olympus.

I waited for Jenni to head off to bed before dialing the Pythia's personal line. When she answered, I could hear happy yapping in the background. It made my heart ache with longing. Saul moseyed into the kitchen, hearing the noise through the phone with his supernatural senses, and laid his head in my lap with a soft whine.

"They're so big!" The Pythia gasped. "And I can definitely see the jackal in them. If Hades catches wind of this, he might just start raising a new hybrid. Jackhound? Hellkal? No. Helljack, perhaps?"

"Wouldn't that be something?" I tried to sound interested while I listened to Coreen and her babies in the background. I wished I could visit one last time, just to scratch her behind the ears and ruffle the fur along her back, even though she kind of hated it. She knew I only did it because I loved her.

The Pythia droned on excitedly. "You should really jump in on that while you have the chance. Make him split profits with you for discovering the majestic pairing."

"Definitely." I tilted my beer back and rolled my eyes.

"You know—" She paused for a moment. "I almost thought you were Grim calling about my prophecy conundrum again."

I coughed, swallowing hard as I sat up straighter on my barstool. "Sorry, what was that? I missed what you said."

She made a reluctant sound in the back of her throat. "My visions are all wonky this year. I mean, I've had rough spells before, but never anything like this. It's like I can't see past the next five minutes, let alone predict Eternity's needs for the next year. Grim has been a real ass about it, too."

"Oh. Sorry." I didn't know what else to say.

"Maybe I'm getting too old for this." She gasped in horror. "What if Apollo trades me in for another oracle?"

"That will never happen," I assured her. Apollo had gone so far as to have a replica of her temple in the mortal realm built for her in the afterlife.

"Well, I'm being summoned to the adytum early tonight. Apollo thinks foreplay is the best way to refine my divination."

"Oh. Okay. Have fun?"

"Of course." She snorted out a giggle and hung up.

My conversations with the Pythia were different each time we spoke. Her personality went through seasons, the same as Apollo's, and when winter struck, the sweet couple pulled a Jekyll and Hyde, morphing into Dionysus and his Maenad.

Apollo's grief over Josie's death had almost caused an apocalypse in its own right when he tried to invoke the winter god a few months early, before communing with the Pythia so she could make her annual predictions for Grim.

The boss man relied on her foresight in order to wisely distribute the soul matter each year. Now that I thought about it, other than being a grade-A tycoon, there was really nothing he contributed to the machine that was Eternity. He just knew how to keep everyone useful in his pocket, through secrets and deception. Anyone who found him out seemed to find their way to the top of his shit list, like Maalik and me.

I let the thought slide. There was no use seething over things I couldn't change, not when none of it would make any difference after Saturday. Death was quite the equalizer.

I emptied the rest of my beer in the sink and threw the bottle away before fixing a turkey sandwich for Kevin, layering on the mayonnaise extra thick as I recalled how easily I was able to count his ribs.

When I poked my head into his room, he was curled up on his freshly made bed, flipping through one of Josie's books with weepy eyes.

"I'm not going to have to box up the books too, am I?" I said grievously.

Kevin snapped the book closed and set in on the nightstand. "No. It's okay." His eyes fell on the plate, and he shook his head. "I'm not really hungry."

"You're a stiff breeze away from being a kite. Eat it." I set the plate down on the end of his bed and folded my arms.

Kevin frowned, but he obligingly picked up the sandwich and took a bite. "Thanks," he mumbled.

"Now." I patted my leg and waited for Saul to pad down the hall and nuzzle in next to me. "We've made some progress tonight, but I don't think you're out of the woods yet. I want to trust you, but after the thieving, you're going to have to earn it. That's going to take time. Meanwhile, I'll be relying on my insurance policy."

Kevin swallowed the bite of sandwich and gave me a confused look. "You mean like renters' insurance?"

"I mean like canine insurance." I glanced down at Saul and pointed to Kevin. "*Detineo.*"

Saul barked, letting me know he understood the Latin command to detain Kevin. Kevin understood it, too.

His frown deepened as he took another bite of his sandwich. "I wasn't planning on going anywhere," he said with his mouth full.

"Now I don't have to worry about it." I shrugged and gave him a tired smile. "See you in the morning."

I headed back to my bedroom and shuffled around in front of the window a bit before clicking off the lights. Then I peeked through the blinds, scanning the street below for any movement. I waited another twenty minutes, just in case Maalik had run off to check the throne realm one last time, and then flipped Winston's coin.

In the blink of space between our two realms, I crossed my fingers, hoping and praying that I'd be the only one on Winston's sunny lawn when I arrived.

CHAPTER TWENTY-FOUR

*"The greatest deception men suffer
is from their own opinions."*
—Leonardo da Vinci

"This realm is boring," Morgan complained. She was slumped in the middle of Winston's oversized couch, her legs kicked out in a very unladylike manner, sending her tutu up in all directions. "There's no night. No wind. No rain. No birds."

"They're frivolous commodities that Grim would not approve. He thought the soul matter was of better use elsewhere," Winston said dully. His appearance was a little tidier than the last time I'd seen him, but he still looked disheartened and exhausted.

"I rather like the simple consistency of it," Father Ron, the priest soul, said from his perch on the arm of the couch. "Though I can imagine one might find it rather drab if they're accustomed to more colorful surroundings."

Winston grunted in agreement.

Everyone seemed like they were getting along, all in all, for which I was thankful. I had enough problems without having to play principal with a bunch of indignant souls. Maalik had been visiting around the clock, so I was told, and he had delivered a few things to keep everyone happy, including a rosary for the priest made by the Virgin herself, and a box of honey cakes from Nessa's donut shop for Morgan.

"The angel tells me he's in possession of the tracking device," Winston said, running a hand up and down his arm as if he were cold, even though the fireplace crackled with flames, filling the cottage with a fragrant warmth.

I nodded. "It appears I'm everyone's favorite reaper to blackmail. If there was an award for that, it'd be mine, hands down."

Winston had enough wits about him to look ashamed. "I'm sorry for the way I behaved. I'm terrified for Naledi, but I shouldn't have taken it out on you."

"Apology accepted."

"I still think you're better suited to rescue her," he added. "The angel doesn't even know what she looks like."

I grabbed the poker by the fireplace and knelt down to dig around in the soot. "I know, but the device doesn't seem to be working properly anyway."

Winston sat down beside Morgan and snatched one of the honey cakes out of the pastry box in her lap. "What I'm having the most trouble with is the bird that visited you," he said to her, shoving the cake into his mouth before she could protest.

"We've been over this a hundred times." She closed the lid of the box. "The fey are honest, almost to a fault. They do not lie—"

"But they don't always tell the truth either," Winston injected.

Morgan glared at him. "They do not lie," she repeated through gritted teeth. "So, they are also less likely to suspect others of lying. Besides, the bird seemed honest enough to me."

Father Ron shook his head. "I still find all of this quite hard to follow, and I'm more than a little put out that my faith was not unanimous beyond the grave. All the war and bickering over whose god took precedence and to find that they all exist and confer on the other side? Well, it makes one feel like a right fool."

"Not *all* of them care for conferring, unfortunately," I grumbled under my breath.

It didn't seem like there was any way to pull Winston aside to talk privately with him. The walls were thin, and the realm was tiny, and since no one besides Maalik interacted with the other two souls anyway, I decided it wouldn't matter if they heard what I had to say next.

"I assume Maalik told you about the soul who attacked Reapers Inc.?"

The priest paled. "I thought he was making up a story to encourage obedience."

"I didn't," Morgan chirped. "The bird did say things were dire in the city." She seemed quite pleased to be in the know.

I set the poker back on the rack and held my hands up to the fire, feeling them tingle from the heat, similar to the way they did when I lost control. "Did Maalik tell you that the soul's message was for me?"

The news silenced Morgan and Father Ron, but Winston leaned forward on the couch, his eyes sinking into me. "Was it about Naledi? Is she okay?"

"The rebels want to make an exchange."

"Yes, yes," the priest snapped, waving his fingers in an agitated circle. "We know there was a riddle, but the angel doesn't seem to understand its entirety. He didn't repeat it verbatim, but we at least understood they were looking for this soul—this Naledi. But the message was for you? You're sure?"

"He didn't tell you?" I snorted. "Of course he didn't."

Winston folded his hands together. "Please, tell me you know something more."

"I know where they want to make the exchange tomorrow night," I said, standing to stretch my legs. "I don't think they have Naledi—"

"Or they do and just don't know who she is," Winston said. He stood and walked over to stand beside me at the fireplace. "She's very clever. She would know not to reveal her position."

I shrugged. "There's no way of knowing for sure."

"Yes, there is." His eyes widened, and I felt something tighten in the pit of my stomach.

"You can't be serious," the priest gave him a withering look, but Winston's eyes never left mine.

"It's my choice. If you knew Naledi, you would understand."

I had planned this, and even though Winston knew what he was volunteering for, I felt guilty for planting the seed.

Some part of me knew that Naledi wasn't with the rebels, but I didn't try any harder to convince Winston.

I should have. It would have been the right thing to do. But, somewhere out there, Bub was waiting for me, and now I had the means to come for him.

CHAPTER TWENTY-FIVE

"There are two things a person should never be angry at,
what they can help, and what they cannot."
—*Plato*

I woke up Friday morning with my heart feeling as if it had spent the night in a vise. I was covered in sweat, and though I couldn't recall my nightmares, a flutter in my stomach told me I must have had plenty.

I rolled over to find Saul's big, dopey face lying on the pillow beside me. His black eyes twinkled as if he had been waiting for me to wake up, and he licked the tip of my nose.

"Eww," I said, running my hand down the front of his muzzle. I scratched his belly and tickled the pads of his paws, big and squishy like stale campfire marshmallows. He yapped and leapt off the bed, prancing over to my side to play tug-of-war with the blankets until I caved and got up.

Kevin was already in the kitchen, fiddling with the coffee pot. "I forget. How many scoops go in?" he asked, his hands shaking.

I circled the counter and took the pot from him. "I'll get it. Would you mind feeding Saul?"

Kevin shuffled over to the coat closet, casting a gloomy expression at the bags of Josie's belongings lined up against the wall, while I set up the coffeemaker and rinsed the muddy ring of coffee Jenni had left in the bottom of the carafe before refilling it with fresh water.

Kevin seemed irritable, but I could tell he was trying. He felt like a different person to me, especially with his boot camp hairdo. We didn't say much as we drank our coffee, parting ways soon after to get ready for the long day—possibly our last one on the job together. As traumatic as it had been to get here, I was glad we had. I was thankful to have this time with him.

We left the condo with Josie's things in tow, stopping off at the storage unit to put them away. When we finished, I had Kevin and Saul accompany me to the office. Kevin made my life easier for a change and didn't protest. I wasn't ready to let him out of my sight, and I could only rely on Saul to babysit to a certain degree.

As we stepped off the elevator, Ellen balked at Kevin's frail physique and buzzed head. She didn't say anything, but she did slide a few extra chocolates across the counter with my soul docket. After a passing glance, I realized that the treats probably had more to do with the abundance of souls on the list rather than the lack of meat on Kevin's bones.

"What the hell is this?" I held the docket up and dropped it back on her desk. The clipboard it was attached to clattered loudly, and Ellen gave me an apologetic grimace.

"Grim wants to see you before you take off." She leaned over her desk and nodded down at Saul. "You might want to have your apprentice take him back to your office and wait," she added in a hushed voice.

Kevin sulked off down the hall, looking like a scolded toddler. He probably thought my meeting with Grim was over his latest guard run-in, but something told me the kid hadn't even made it onto the boss man's radar. I pointed Saul after Kevin, and he dutifully followed.

"Poor kid." Ellen shook her head and sighed. "How you holdin' up, sweetie?"

I shrugged and rolled my eyes, trying to keep them from watering as my thoughts lingered on Josie. I didn't need to be a sappy mess for what I was getting ready to walk into. "What's Grim want?" I asked sharply, snatching up the docket again. "Is he planning on explaining this?"

Ellen's face puckered as she pushed the intercom button on her desk phone. "Captain Harvey is here, sir."

"Send her in," Grim's gravelly voice demanded, crackling through the intercom and muffling through his office door simultaneously.

I gave Ellen a sour look for her duck-and-cover maneuver and braced myself before entering Grim's office.

"Close the door," he grumbled, pushing his chair away from his desk and a heap of paperwork. "And sit down."

I gave the office door a shove and sat down on one of the torturously uncomfortable chairs spread out before Grim's desk. Most might mistake them for guests, but that would imply they were comfortable. There was no doubt in my mind that someone had designed these specifically to make people feel unwelcome.

Grim stood and sat on the edge of his desk so he could look down at me. It was a psychological move to imply his looming superiority, and it was unnecessary. Mouthing off might have been my inclination once upon a time, but that was before I'd seen him in action—behind the scenes and on the battlefield. As much as I reviled Grim, there was a certain degree of respect that came with fear.

He stared silently at me for a long, tedious moment before speaking. "No brilliant insights happened to come to you since our last meeting, I take it?"

"Sorry," I mumbled, shaking my head.

He fell quiet again, his eyes glued to mine in an unnerving stalemate. Did he think he would develop x-ray vision if he squinted long and hard enough? The desk creaked under his weight as he shifted, and the spell was broken. "I'm sending a guard with you today."

"Why?" I asked slowly, trying not to sound like a disgruntled teenager.

Grim gave me a weary look. "Do you want the PC version or the hard truth?"

I raised my eyebrows, aiming for innocent surprise, but he was having none of it.

"The rebels are sending you messages. You're clearly in danger. The council sees fit to offer you protection due to your previous *good deeds*." He snorted.

Rats. I almost swung my fist in a comic arch and blurted "foiled again." But if I could only go down once, it wouldn't be at the hands of this shmuck.

It took me a moment to spot it, but Grim had made one tiny mistake in his PC rambling. "*Messages*? As in, more than one?"

The victorious sneer melted from his face. "Your escort is waiting downstairs." He stood and circled his desk. I hesitated, my mouth opening to inquire further, and he growled, "Get out." There was no use sticking around after that dismissal.

Grim wouldn't be sharing any more details, and I already knew what the hard truth of the situation was. He was afraid I'd try to snag the throne soul and rescue Bub.

Keeping an eye on me seemed like a good way to curb my itch—and withholding another message from the rebels seemed like a dirty move, too. There was only one other person who would know what the message was, but I had a feeling he wouldn't play nice either.

In my frustration and anxious ignorance, I had completely forgotten to bitch about the monstrous harvest list. I was pretty sure that had been intentional, too. Anything to keep me occupied today.

Even if the whole unit, Kevin included, hauled ass, we were going to be harvesting souls well past nightfall. The small flicker of hope I'd been clinging to dimmed, damn near burning out, but as I walked past the break room with its slew of cheesy motivational posters, I was struck with an insanely brilliant idea.

Kevin and Saul perked up as I entered my office. I held up a finger when Kevin stood, signaling him to give me a minute, and flipped open my cellphone. I punched in Warren's number and pressed my lips together until he answered.

"I don't think I can wait until next week," I said, breathing excitedly. "I wanna take the bike out now."

CHAPTER TWENTY-SIX

*"Individual commitment to a group effort—that is what
makes a team work, a company work,
a society work, a civilization work."*
—Vince Lombardi

I don't know why Grim bothered to send a guard when Maalik was still in stalker-mode. I had to wonder if there was a bug in my phone when the angel met us at Holly House. His wings were ruffled and damp as if he'd cut his morning shower short just to ruin my day.

"You're not licensed to drive that in Limbo City," he insisted, shifting his menacing scowl between Warren and me at the mouth of the garage. I was straddling the bike a mere ten feet from Divine Boulevard, ready to take on the world.

"Good thing I won't be cruising around Limbo then," I said, flicking a feather off my shoulder. Saul snapped at it playfully as it drifted to the garage floor, sending Kevin back a step.

"She's quite competent," Warren said, his wings shrinking below his shoulders as Maalik's death glare fixated on him.

"What's the big deal?" I revved the motor to draw his attention again. "I'm going three blocks. My *babysitter* can fly."

I nodded at the nephilim perched on the garage roof. "Both of them," I added, giving Maalik a knowing smirk.

His chest puffed out, but his cheeks had a shameful glow. He had totally bugged my phone. I thought back to all the times he'd steered me around by the elbow. It would have been an easy trick to manage.

I shifted the weight of the bike to my opposite leg and cleared my throat. "Don't you have somewhere better to be, councilor?"

"Lana." He always looked so pained when I played the formality card. "This is too dangerous. You're being reckless." I had a feeling he wasn't just talking about the bike.

"I know what I'm doing." I looked over my shoulder at Kevin and jerked my head at the bike. "Hop on, grasshopper."

He slipped off his robe and wadded it up, placing it in one of the leather saddlebags Warren had fitted on the bike since my last practice session. Maalik watched as he climbed on behind me, but the wrath in his expression had deflated.

"You have a death wish, don't you?" He shook his head with a defeated sigh.

I wanted to ask if it really mattered at this point, but there was no need to spoil Warren's and Kevin's last days, too.

"Catch you on the flipside," I said, throwing Maalik a sarcastic salute before pulling out onto the street.

Kevin's chest bumped my back, and he let out a little gasp as his hands timidly groped my hips and waist, looking for a kosher place to hold on. Saul barreled down the sidewalk beside us, his ears and tongue flopping happily. I could never keep up when we went running, and he was often reduced to jogging laps around me. He seemed glad for the opportunity to blow off the cobwebs.

Traffic had picked up a little, but nothing like it used to be during the week of the ball. The bike drew a few glances, but no one else tried to put a kink in my plans—not even Abe, the nephilim tailing me on Grim's orders.

I liked Abe. This wasn't his first time playing bodyguard for me, and I was sure that's why Grim had chosen him. I had respect for the guy, and I'd felt more than a little guilty when Loki had bludgeoned him unconscious in order to hoodwink me last summer. Sure, it wasn't really my fault, and I was bludgeoned unconscious by the same douchebag shortly after. I didn't know if that made us even, but I would definitely feel bad when it came time to give Abe the slip.

I tilted one of my side view mirrors up to watch him, wiggling my fingers in a carefree wave when he caught me.

When we reached the harbor, I drove the bike right down the dock and up the ramp to my ship.

"Sweet Jesus!" Tyler walked a circle around us. "I want one." When Abe landed on the quarterdeck railing, Tyler jumped and stumbled back to stand beside Molly.

Arden gave the guard a curious frown, while Kate and Alex pretended not to notice him at all, choosing to nervously focus on belly-rubbing Saul instead.

"Today is fucked," I announced. There was no time for sugarcoating or apologies, so I cut right to the chase. "Grim is an asshole, and contrary to popular belief, he doesn't think much of me either. Harvests are going to run into the witching hours tonight, but if you can hang in there with me, I'll buy the first round at Purgatory once we finish up."

Abe's wings rustled at my crass tone. His eyes darted around suspiciously as I passed out the individual dockets as if surprised that no one was offended by my reward.

My unit knew how I felt about the false accusations directed at Xaph's bar, and even on their bad days, they were compassionate freethinkers. I'd bought them a round at Purgatory before, right after the worst of the media's smear campaign had infected the city. I was no crusader for the Demon Suffrage Movement, but I'd be damned if I would stand aside and watch a friend's business go belly-up because of a bunch of brainless jerks after an easy target.

When everyone except Kevin and I had coined off, I motioned Abe down to give him a copy of our agenda with detailed coordinates. His nose curled up at the list, but he fished a coin out of a gap in his armor and prepared to follow us.

Kevin joined me on the bike again, and Saul trailed us down to the dock, brushing up against my leg so our auras could connect. I put a coin in the slot on the bike's dash and entered the coordinates for our first harvest, a food poisoning incident in Colorado.

"You really think we'll get through all that today?" Kevin asked, his brow creasing as he peeked over my shoulder and scanned the docket.

I shrugged and tucked the clipboard down in a saddlebag. "Gonna have to," I said, kicking the bike into gear and giving the throttle a quick twist.

The coin in the dash began to spin, and I winced a little as the tally marks along the edge faded. Between the bike, two reapers, and a hellhound, the travel expense was going to hurt today. I eased off the clutch, and we pulled forward, out of one realm and into the next.

Saul yipped, tickled by the show. Abe appeared a moment later, looking a bit flustered and uncertain about our location. As a nephilim, I doubted he spent much time on this side. He perched atop a streetlight in front of the hospital where half a dozen bodies waited for us inside.

One of the best things about being a reaper was not being visible to living humans. Souls couldn't see us until they were stripped of their mortal flesh—except for a very rare few born with the sight and original believers. I could count on one hand the number of those I'd encountered in my three hundred years.

Seeing as how my bike was crafted Eternity-side, it was invisible too, so I didn't have to worry about thieves if I left it on the street. Still, I pocketed the keys and dug the coin out of the dash. Then I remembered what Warren had said about the coin dial and popped it out of the console too before venturing inside the hospital. My luck had been shit for long enough that I knew when not to take chances.

Abe followed Kevin and me at a safe distance. Saul hung back too, keeping Abe company and staying out of our way until summoned.

It was an easy enough harvest. The list had been long, not dumb and dangerous, and though I'd split the jobs up hastily, I'd paid enough attention to group them according to location. Our next stop was just a city over, a highway pileup. If we coined the first lot of souls off to the ship fast enough, we could make it back in time before the ambulances arrived, now that we were riding in style.

Kevin was doing remarkably well, keeping his head down and reaping like a pro. Yet I still worried about him more and more as the day drew on. There was a twitch in his right eye when he thought I wasn't looking, and he zoned out on occasion, staring raptly at the sky as if he could see things that weren't actually there. I could tell he needed more than I had to offer, and it pained me.

After our sixth and largest harvest, consisting of several dozen victims in a massive ice storm along the east coast, Abe finally tired of shadowing us and opted to stay with the bike on the mortal side while we ran soul lots back and forth to the ship. Grim would have had a fit if he'd known, and Maalik too, which reassured me that the broody angel had finally pissed off to do whatever he did when he wasn't being a pain in my ass.

After two final harvests, we all returned to the ship looking like something the hellcat had dragged in. The sky had faded to a dark, cobalt blue over Limbo City. Wispy, gray and purple clouds streaked through a smear of pink along the horizon that glowed and reflected off the sea, reaching out toward the harbor. A dozen foreign ships crowded the end pier of the dock, more than likely belonging to ball-goers.

I parked the bike on the deck of my ship, looping a coil of rope around it and the main mast just in case we hit any turbulence. Kevin raced around prepping the sails. He seemed less agitated when his hands were busy.

"What are you doing?" Abe asked, swooping down next to me as I finished tying off the bike.

I pulled the keys and coin dial, stuffing them down into my bag. "Warren will kill me if I bring this thing back with a scratch on it."

"Not that," Abe grumbled, removing his crested helmet. "I mean with the souls. You have to deliver them all tonight?" He looked downright miserable, even more so when Kevin shoved off from the dock. "Won't the gates be closed by now?"

"I wish. Of course, you don't have to come with us if—"

"You know I do." The corners of his mouth pulled down until his chin wrinkled.

"Suit yourself." I shrugged, trying to feign disinterest. "There's a fridge in the navigation room off the quarterdeck. We keep it stocked with treats if you get snacky." Abe folded his arms as if he knew I was up to something. I rolled my eyes. "We're on the sea, and I don't have wings like you do. Where exactly do you think I'm going?"

He nodded to the tender boat suspended off the port side of the ship. The starboard tender was in the shop getting a new battery, so we were down to just the one. I was fairly certain Abe could keep up with the electric motor without breaking a sweat. It wasn't part of the plan, and truthfully, I hadn't even considered it.

I gave Abe a tired sigh and reached inside the boat, yanking the keys from the ignition. I held them out with two fingers and dropped them into his open hand. "Happy?" I raised an eyebrow. "Help yourself to a cupcake. I'm going to take a nap. It's an hour to Summerland."

"A nap? Where?" The guy just didn't quit.

"The bed in my cabin. Where else?"

He fluttered after me down the back hallway. "I'll have to clear the room first."

"And check if there are any inflatable lifeboats stashed under my bed?" I laughed.

"Grim's orders were very clear."

"I'll bet they were."

Once Abe gave the green light, I locked myself in the cabin. It wouldn't buy me a lot of time, but I'd take what I could get. I ripped a piece of stationery off a pad on the desk and scribbled out a quick note to Kevin. I wanted to say so much more to him than there was time for, but I did my best.

I left the note on the desk, weighing it down with a heavy coin. Money was the least of my worries right now, and I'd promised the unit a round after work anyway. I left my phone in the desk, too. The last thing I needed was Maalik foiling my plan before it even took off.

There hadn't been a chance to gear up before Grim cramped my style with one of his feathered minions, so all I had to rely on was what I had in my bag—the strap of throwing stars and half a can of angelica mace. There was also a hunting knife tucked in my right boot. I rarely left home without it anymore. It wasn't much, but it would do in a pinch.

I dug Winston's large coin out of my pocket, gave the room one last look, and then pulled the magic trick of the year. Grim was going to be pissed.

The three souls were waiting for me out on the lawn of the throne realm when I appeared. The perma-noon sunlight beat down on us, failing to invoke the carefree picnic mood it usually did. Morgan and Father Ron stood on either side of Winston, looks of grave concern staining their faces.

"This all seems so unnecessary." Father Ron said. "Even as a mere restorer of faith, your life has value."

Morgan nodded sadly as she untied her stone necklace and tucked it into Winston's hand. "If you change your mind, don't hesitate to use it. Just a half twist."

Winston smiled and kissed the top of her head, while I furiously paced ruts in the grass. "Maalik's going to be here any second," I hissed softly, taking a deep breath as I wiped my sweaty palms down the front of my jeans.

"You're right." Father Ron let out a little gasp. "What should we tell him?"

"Uh, nothing." I couldn't believe this guy.

"Nothing?" He blinked at me a moment as if he didn't understand the word. "But dear Winston will be gone. The angel will demand an explanation."

"You expect us to lie?" Morgan sounded horrified, but the twinkle in her eyes told me she was already thinking of a clever, fey way around the question.

"Tell him you didn't *see* where Winston disappeared to," I said through gritted teeth, my patience slipping dangerously close to the tingly wrath threshold.

"Oh. Yes, I think that wording would help you around your fey nature, Morgan." The priest's eyes lit, and he nodded. "That reminds me. I forgot to ask. Where *are* you going?"

"If I told you that, then you *would* have to lie."

Winston finally wandered over close enough, and I snagged his shoulder. He jumped in surprise. We exchanged a look, the kind that didn't happen often.

It spanned everything, from the very beginning when I had harvested him as a dying child in an American hospital, through his past lives regression back to King Tut, the child king who had also died young, and now as this new entity of his own creation. He was still too young to tempt fate, but it seemed like a tic of his soul. I wondered if any of his other lives had made it past twenty. I felt the urge to talk him down again. This was the fork in the road, and there wouldn't be another chance.

Winston made the call before I could second-guess what we were about to do. He reached his hand up to take my shoulder, mirroring my hold on him, and flipped a coin.

The soft grass slithered away, fading beneath the rocky terrain of the Tartarus mountain range overlooking the ruins of the summer manor. The viewing ledge was just around the bend, and right behind that was the cave where I had pressed my bloody palm after my last meeting with Bub.

A peak marked in fool's blood.

This was it. Now, we waited.

CHAPTER TWENTY-SEVEN

"Panic causes tunnel vision.
Calm acceptance of danger allows us to more easily assess the situ-
ation and see the options."
—Simon Sinek

Winston's foot nudged mine again, and I reached my hand out to push him back in the shadow of the mountain, my eyes still focused on the viewing ledge.

"You're moving around too much," I whispered. "The element of surprise could be our saving grace tonight, but not if you can't stand still for more than five seconds."

"Sorry," he muttered, heaving an audible sigh that made me question his sincerity.

"Remember, not a word when they arrive. You have to look disheartened and unwilling. Any eagerness on your part, and the game is up." I stole a quick glance to make sure he was listening.

Winston scratched at his wrist, holding it close to his face as he turned it over in the scant starlight. He'd exchanged Morgan's necklace for a tracking bracelet once we left the throne realm. The rebels were elusive enough without getting their hands on anything else that granted invisibility.

Reclaiming the Helm of Hades over the summer had been a nightmare.

Winston poked his wrist. He seemed disturbed by the way the bracelet had dissolved and disappeared under his ghostly skin.

I cleared my throat and pushed him back against the mountain again with a frown. "And you'll definitely have to knock that off."

He blushed and tucked his hands back in his sleeves before folding them against his stomach.

Our black robes seemed to melt into the shadows, and as long as we were perfectly still, I was hopeful that whatever rebel had been tasked with making the exchange wouldn't see us coming. It wasn't that I had some clever assault planned, but I wouldn't put it past Seth's minions. If they could get the jump on me, it was well within character for them to snatch Winston and slit Bub's throat.

If they hadn't already.

The thought soured my stomach, and it had crossed my mind more than once, but even the slimmest chance that their offer was genuine wrenched my heart.

It had been nearly two months since I'd last seen Bub, on this very mountain. The fact that the rebels knew about the blood I'd memorialized our last night with roused a whole new slew of awful possibilities.

Could they have been watching him even then? Has he been their prisoner this whole time? Or did they torture the information out of him? I pushed away the idea that he might have jumped the fence and swore fealty to a scab like Seth.

There was no way he would turn on me. I had to believe that, or else what was I doing here?

It was pushing midnight when I finally heard movement up on the viewing ledge. The can of angelica mace was rolled in the cuff of my sleeve, and I'd slit my robe up one side so I could access the throwing stars if I needed them.

The shuffle of feet grew louder. Winston heard it too and trembled beside me.

"Are you ready?" I mouthed, looking squarely at him for what I hoped wouldn't be the last time.

The starry night reflected in his wide eyes as if the entire universe resided in his soul, and I hated myself for agreeing to this. He nodded solemnly.

We crept around the corner, me pushing Winston forward, him breathing harder, working up to the panicked outrage I had requested he invoke. He stumbled on the rocky terrain, and I had to force myself to remain unmoved as if he were truly just a bargaining chip. Any weakness shown to the rebels was torture fodder, and I'd already given them enough.

The rebel liaison, though I saw her first, took me by surprise. The succubus leaned against the mountainside, her pinky-less hand grasping her naked hip, a smug grin tight across her face. "I knew you'd fall for my little show. Admit it. You needed the extra push, didn't you? The witch tends to go a little overboard with the riddles, and the insiders tell me you never even saw the pound of flesh we left on Grim's doorstep."

I held Winston's shoulder firmly, keeping my eyes open for any movement in the darkness surrounding the ledge.

"Where's Bub? I have a coin in hand, and unless I see him in the next two seconds, we're gone."

The succubus pouted at me as if she had planned on gloating a while longer. Then she reached one of her scaly arms inside the cave and pulled Bub out into the open.

He looked horrible, even in the dim light. His hands were bound behind his back, and his bare chest was covered in a crosshatch pattern of cuts and welts. Some bled, and others oozed with infection. One of his black pant legs had been torn away, and it looked like something had gnawed through his calf all the way to the bone.

I searched his face, hoping for some sign that he was glad to see me, but his eyes were swollen and shadowed. A coarse gag wrapped around his head, cutting into the corners of his lips and prying his jaws open, and crusty blood flaked around the stubble on his chin. He staggered as the succubus shook his arm.

"Ta-da!" she sang. She grabbed a handful of his hair and jerked his head back over her shoulder, running her black tongue up the side of his throat. "One last taste, lover," she purred at him.

I tried to look away, tried to curb my passion until the exchange was complete, but it was no use. "Do you want the soul or not?" I snapped.

Winston shuddered under my hand. I felt bad for him, but not half as bad as I felt for Bub. If the kid changed his mind on me now, I wasn't sure I could back down. Not with the way Bub looked.

The succubus pouted again. "You're no fun. No wonder fly boy here was so eager to ditch you for the dark side."

The fear that she was stalling sent my pulse into overdrive. My eyes flickered to the shadow of the cave, where it was likely a second agent waited. I needed to take control of the situation. Fast.

"Here's how we're doing this," I said. "I'm going to walk the soul over, and you're going to take your hands off Beelzebub as soon as I reach you."

"Really?" She snickered. "You think you're in charge now, little girl?"

I lifted my coin for her to see. "How thrilled will Seth be if he finds out I showed with the soul, and you screwed it up?"

She cocked her head. "Oh, I don't think you'd go to all this trouble to fetch your lover boy just to leave him behind."

"I don't know," I sighed. "The thought of Seth eating your eyeballs for being a fuckup is pretty satisfying."

Her smirk tightened as her fingernails dug into Bub's shoulder, provoking a stifled grunt. I trained my eyes on the succubus's face, ignoring the stabbing sensation in my chest, and gave my coin a quick, single roll between my first two fingers.

"Fine! Have it your way," she barked, her eyes widening at the coin. I didn't give her a chance to recover.

The stars shone brighter along this side of the mountain, and Winston kept his footing this time. I could feel his pulse under my hand as I squeezed his shoulder, my last attempt to reassure him that everything would be fine. Unless his bracelet was as defunct as Naledi's.

Maalik had the tracking compact, so there was no way to run a test to be sure any of the bracelets worked. We were taking a huge leap of faith here, but the time for doubts had long passed. I quieted my mind, focusing entirely on the exchange. I could dwell over regrets later.

I caught movement in the corner of my eye, from somewhere above the cave opening, but I didn't turn to take a better look. Once we were about ten feet away, I saw the movement again. I'd seen enough westerns to know an ambush when I was walking into one.

I leaned in closer to Winston. "We got company. Any of your past lives play football?" I whispered. He squared up his shoulders and gave me the slightest of nods. "Then have at it."

Winston took off, darting to the right and slipping past the succubus. She let go of Bub to reach for the kid, but he was too fast. About the same time, a harpy swooped down from her poorly hidden perch. Her tarry, winged arms flapped murderously, blocking the mountain path as she screeched in Winston's face.

The rebel hags looked triumphant, and I guess they were. But so was I. Before either of them knew what had happened, I slipped my arm around Bub's waist and rolled my coin twice more.

The mountain bled out of sight, and we collapsed on the harbor dock. The lanterns were blinding, but I managed to wrestle Bub's bruised and bloodied body into the shadow of a yacht. My ship was just up the pier, but a careful glance revealed a pair of nephilim on the neighboring vessel. They were staking out my boat. *Shit.*

I had only half expected the exchange to be successful, but that was enough to make me feel like a supreme idiot for not planning any further ahead.

I scooted back into the shadow of the yacht and turned to Bub. His face was wet with tears, causing the dried blood on his skin to melt into a muddy mess. His breath rasped around the gag.

I dug the hunting knife out of my boot and, as gently as I could, wedged it under the rough fabric. It made a soft pop as I cut it free. Bub opened and closed his mouth slowly as if relearning how it worked, while I sawed through the bindings on his hands.

"What have you done?" he whispered, the words coming out in a broken slur. I could tell it hurt just to breathe.

"I love you," I said as if that explained everything. I turned one of Bub's hands over in mine and bent to kiss the rope burn along his wrist.

His breath hissed out slowly. "My sacrifice is worth nothing if you hand Eternity over to the rebels."

"Sacrifice, shmacrifice."

That earned a soft chuckle. "How I've missed your sweet nothings."

I tried to smile, but I could feel the tears burning to reach my eyes. I ran a hand over my forehead. "My ship isn't safe, but I think I know where we might be able to go."

Bub's face darkened. "You shouldn't have come. Arma-geddon—" He coughed, spilling blood from the corner of his mouth.

"Armageddon can wait. The ceremony isn't until tomor-row."

"Tomorrow? One day?" His eyes widened, and I noticed the white of one was shot through with blood, the lid black and swollen.

"I'd do it all again just to have one more day with you."

Bub smiled weakly. His charm was still intact, even if he was broken and bruised. "Where to, love?"

I grinned and rubbed my teary cheek against my shoulder. "The dock mechanic's station is a pier over. Think you can make it?"

He nodded.

I stood and helped pull him upright, grunting under his weight as I wrapped one of his arms over my shoulders. His breath rasped out through his nose as he put pressure on his mangled leg, but he tried to work with me, sluggishly steady-ing himself on a dock post.

"We're going to have to be quick and quiet. They're watching my ship," I said, straining quietly as we staggered down the dock.

Bub didn't answer, too focused on putting one foot in front of the other. Once we stepped out of the yacht's shadow, I quickened our pace, not daring to look back toward my ship.

My boots thumped softly on the dock floor, while Bub's bare feet hardly made a sound, though they did leave a faint trail of blood in our wake. The glaring lanterns threw our shadows in all directions, creating a flurry of motion that wasn't likely to go unnoticed.

By the time we reached the mechanic's pier, my breath burned in my lungs, and my pulse ached in my ears. Bub's face was a mask of red determination.

"Who goes there?" a guard shouted behind us.

Wings flapped violently in the air, but I'd already spotted my starboard tender. The small boat was laid across a dock lift, the battery cables twisted and reaching for the sky.

I lifted Bub's injured leg, crooking my elbow under his knee. "Jump!" He didn't question the order.

We landed hard against the pulley platform in the center of the boat and fell back onto one of the bench seats.

"Halt!" another guard shouted, closer this time.

"What are you doing?" Bub asked, his voice hitched with panic as I dug around in my bag.

My hand closed around the coin dial I'd taken off Warren's bike. I pulled it out with a whispery, manic laugh, waving it in the air as if it were the Holy Grail. The first hint of uncertainty crossed Bub's face.

I slapped the dial onto the pulley platform of the boat and twisted the coin in its slot. "Hang on to your britches, fly boy."

He cringed. "Please don't call me that."

The flap of nephilim wings was closer than ever, and a slender, white feather drifted down between Bub and me. It floated there for a second and then zipped out of existence as the boat jolted off the lift.

The lantern light was replaced by the subtle glow of the moon as the boat landed with a grating clunk against a hillside. Bub groaned at the impact. His shoulders trembled as he grasped the edge of the boat, leaning over the edge with a sickly expression.

"We made it," I sighed, unable to suppress a nervous laugh. I pulled my robe over my head and stuffed it into my bag before stashing it under one of the bench seats. Then I flopped out of the boat and landed on my side in the sandy soil.

The rush of waves to shore drew Bub's eyes out across the sea just a few yards away. "Made it where?"

"The Sea of Avalon." I grunted as I put all my weight into dragging the boat toward the water. Bub tried to climb out, but I stopped him. "It's not far. Stay put."

A breeze carried haunting music across the sea from the island I'd seen the night I met Morgan. The wind played with Bub's hair, and he shivered against it, a soft frown tugging at his wounded mouth.

"You have an open invitation with the fey?" he asked.

"Not exactly," I said, panting as I struggled with the boat. "But I've met one of the fair folk, and I think she'll help us out."

"You're serious?" Bub said, sounding as if he would have preferred taking our chances with the Nephilim Guard.

My boots squished in the soggy soil at the edge of the sea, and I clung to the lip of the boat as I worked my way around to the backside, giving it a good heave into the water before climbing back in.

"We don't have many options, and this is the best I could do. Just don't eat anything they offer."

"I'm not stupid." He blushed as his stomach grumbled.

I gave him a gentle kiss on the cheek, too afraid to test out his mouth yet.

Bub's eyebrows lifted suggestively. "I regret that I'm in no position to ravage you."

"We'll make do," I said, feeling along the floorboard of the boat until I found the paddles. It was too much to hope that the new battery would be installed, but I was certainly glad the bike's coin dial had managed to get the boat here at all.

Even though it was small, the boat was a beast to maneuver manually, so I let Bub help. We paddled out across the dark water, the rippling reflection of the moon and stars encircling us. If we hadn't been nerve-shot and desperate for aid, it might have actually been a romantic moment.

The music grew louder as we approached the isle, cutting off abruptly once we were spotted. Shouts rang out, and the fires along the beach were smothered. A war drum began to beat, quickly joined by another.

Bub gave me a chastising frown. He nodded at the coin dial on the platform. "Will that little device of yours rescue us here?"

I swallowed. "It only worked at the harbor because the boat was on a lift connected to the dock. It wouldn't have done us any good in the water." I looked back at the island, still a quarter of a mile away.

A small boat slipped into the sea. The white garb of the faerie queen glowed in the moonlight, illuminating the archer sitting on the bench ahead of her. The darker elf's bowstring was pulled back, an arrow trained in our direction.

Maybe I had underestimated Una's goodwill.

CHAPTER TWENTY-EIGHT

*"Obsessed by a fairy tale, we spend our lives searching
for a magic door and a lost kingdom of peace."*
—Eugene O'Neill

Una was not pleased with me at all. "Where is my sweet fawn?" she demanded. Her archer was still focused on us, and the arrow in her grasp diverted my attention in a nervously annoying manner.

"She's fine. I assure you," I said, my hands lifted in surrender.

"I didn't ask *how* she was. I asked *where.*" The queen stamped her foot, rocking the small boat, and I flinched. I was just sure the archer would lose her grip on the arrow. She had been holding the same position for at least ten minutes.

"She's staying with another soul. The Oracle Ball is tomorrow, and I'm sure she'll return soon after." It wasn't an outright lie. If the world ended tomorrow, we'd *all* be returning. Back to the great void from whence we came.

Una gave me a penetrating glare. The snake in her headdress even hissed in my direction. "You speak the truth, but how can I be sure my fawn trusts you?"

I kept one eye on the archer and slowly lifted the stone necklace out from under my robe. "Is this proof enough?"

The archer blinked in surprise. She glanced back at Una, lowering her bow when the queen nodded.

"I will grant you one night's rest upon our isle, but you must leave before the first light of morning," she said, unhinging a silvery twig from her crown. She looped a string of leather around it, fashioning a necklace, and handed it to her archer to pass between the boats. "The stone will be enough for you, but the demon must wear this."

"Thank you." I closed my eyes, finally feeling the strangling tension release from my body. When I looked up again, the queen was glaring at me.

"My favors are not free, reaper. You cannot trade with something as worthless as your thanks."

"So I'll owe you one?" I asked, batting away the panic trying to claim me again.

"Indeed." She made a clicking, whistling noise through her teeth, and her boat turned as if on its own and slid back toward the island. Another invisible force took hold of the tender boat and pulled us along behind her.

I turned to Bub, and with careful hands, I tied the twig necklace around his throat, trying to keep it high enough that it wouldn't graze any of the abrasions on his chest.

He stared at me with amused eyes. "You just *thanked* a faerie," he said as if I'd stepped on a cobra's tail.

"So?"

"You warned me about not eating anything, and then you go and thank a faerie."

"Oh." I felt my face flush.

How could I have forgotten? Faeries hated to be thanked. Something about the words dismissing their good deeds. Well, Una certainly made it clear that I wouldn't be dismissing her good deed any time soon. It was hard telling what she'd want in return, but right now, I didn't care. Bub and I had a place to rest up and lick our wounds. Well, they were mostly his, and I'd be doing something more sanitary than licking. The point was, we were safe. At least until morning.

The boats pushed up on the shore, and Una made a sign in the air. Music began playing again, and the fey slipped out of the brush and cover of the trees to resume their dancing and feasting. The fires were relit along the beach.

I grabbed my bag out of the bench seat, along with the coin dial on the platform, before hooking Bub's arm over my shoulders again and exiting the boat.

A tall faerie in a silver dress directed us to a tent at the edge of the patch of woods behind the beach. Inside, decorated rugs were layered over the ground. To the left, a low bed stacked with colorful pillows and velvety throw blankets promised sweet dreams. On the right, a table had been set for two. Platters of bread and cheese, meats and sauces, and mountains of apples crowded the center.

I lowered Bub to one of the chairs, groaning as his weight lifted. He touched the twig at his throat as he glanced over the table. "This means we can eat now, right?"

"It better," I said, taking in the goodies.

A pair of sturdy fey brushed past us as they heaved a tub of steaming water inside the tent. The faerie in the silver dress was close behind. She set a bottle of wine on the table and a large basket of soaps and towels on one of the chairs.

"I will return before sunrise to wake you," she said curtly, then left the tent with the two delivery fey in tow. The queen might have extended a formal invitation, but it didn't mean we were welcomed by everyone here.

"Food first?" I asked Bub, turning around to find him already at the table, a chunk of meat clutched in each hand. His cheeks were bloated, and he swallowed hard at my alarmed expression.

"You said it was okay, didn't you?" he asked as he took another bite.

I wondered how long it had been since the rebels had fed him. From his ravenous shoveling, it seemed like it must have been weeks. I waited until he paused to take a breath before joining him at the table.

"You're going to make yourself sick," I said, picking up an apple. "I have a feeling no one will be by to clear the table, so you can always have more after a bath."

Bub sighed and gave the tub an apprehensive look. "Wine first. I'm going to need something to dull the pain." He uncorked the bottle and poured us both a glass.

I pushed mine away. "You need this more than I do right now."

He didn't argue, quickly polishing off the entire bottle. When he finished, I helped him out of what was left of his pants, paying extra careful attention to the nasty wound on his left calf. Then we hobbled over to the bath.

The water was still hot, maybe too hot, but it would be good for cleaning the wounds. The sweet perfume of salt mixed with tea tree and lavender oils wafted up to greet us. Bub put his good leg in first, moaning as he sank into the delicious concoction. He propped the foot of his ravaged leg along the rim of the tub and leaned back, reclining his head stiffly to keep his battered chest above the water.

I brought the bath basket to the side of the tub and dug through it until I found a washcloth. I dipped it into the water and lifted it to Bub's face, rubbing tender circles over his cheeks and forehead to scrub away the grit and stale blood.

When I moved down to his chest, his hand caught my wrist, and he took a deep, shuddering breath.

"I'll be gentle," I said, pressing a soft kiss to his knuckles.

He released me slowly and closed his eyes, turning his face away.

I squeezed the washcloth over the fresher, smaller cuts first, dabbing at them lightly to make sure the healing water penetrated. Bub winced as the salt worked its way in, but he didn't cry out. Not until I started on the infected gashes. His body trembled under my hands, and I didn't realize I was crying until he reached up to wipe a tear from my cheek.

"They're only flesh wounds," he croaked, casting me a painful grin.

I glanced down at his suspended leg. "That one isn't."

Bub's smile waned. "I was hoping you'd forgotten I had that leg. I really only need the one."

"Are you going to make me do it?" I asked, more tears brimming my lashes.

"No." Bub clenched his teeth. "You better stand back for this one."

"I'll hold your hand," I offered.

He shook his head. "I'm liable to break it, love."

I reluctantly stood and moved back a step. Bub lifted his leg and plunged it in the tub so suddenly that I jumped. A scream tore from his throat that sounded like two, one rough and animalistic, echoing behind a shriller note that was just as inhuman. When it broke, he whimpered and gasped for air, reaching out blindly for me.

I knelt back down beside the tub and took his hand, cradling it to my chest. The water in the tub had taken on a red tint as I cleaned his chest, but now it was darker, and the sweet smell muted.

I waited for Bub to catch his breath. His eyes blinked open and slowly focused on my face. "I'm sorry," he whispered, barely able to choke out the words.

"For what?" I shook my head and lifted his hand to my lips. "None of this is your fault."

"It is," he said, sobbing out a bitter laugh. "You have no idea. I worked so hard on that cover, and the most idiotic of slips—" His face crumpled with shame.

"It doesn't matter. None of it matters now." I kissed his hand. "We're together. Don't let anything else weigh on your mind."

Bub looked up at me. "I don't deserve you."

I shushed him. "None of that. Only happy thoughts tonight."

He sat up straighter, grimacing as he reached his other hand out to cup my face. "I said your name." The skin around his eyes crinkled as if he couldn't believe what he was admitting. "I was…*with* her, and I said your name."

"The succubus?" I lifted an eyebrow, beginning to understand his humiliation. "By *with*, you mean—?" He nodded. No wonder the hag had such a big chip on her shoulder.

I grinned, unable to hide my amusement. "She did all of this to you because you called out my name mid-shag?"

Bub looked horrified. "It was such an amateur error. Cindy would thrash me if she knew."

"Forget Cindy. Forget the succubus. I don't want to talk about either of them. You're mine tonight."

Bub smiled widely, wincing as the cuts in the corners of his mouth pulled. "Even maimed and disgraced, you still want me. I'll say it again. I don't deserve you."

I stood and fetched a chair from the table, dragging it over to the tub. Then I shook out a towel and draped it over the back.

Bub gripped the edge of the tub with one hand and gave me his other. As he stood, red rivulets dripped down the length of his body, bouncing over the ribs that pushed through his flesh. I helped him turn and sit on the chair before he lifted his good leg out.

His injured leg dangled over the tub, leaking darker fluids. Chunks of flesh were missing, and a flap of skin peeled away at his shin, revealing stark bone beneath. It hurt just to look at it.

I kicked off my boots and removed the laces before shaking out another towel and draping it over both arms. Bub nestled his leg in the middle, clenching his teeth and trembling as I fingered his flesh back in place as best I could. I wrapped the towel around his calf, securing it tightly with my boot laces.

Bub stood and wrapped the towel on the chair around his waist, holding it closed with one hand. His hair dripped down the side of his neck and pooled above his collarbone and in the hollow of his throat. I'd thought being clean would make him look better, maybe less abused, but he was emaciated.

I took his free arm and walked him to the bed. The fey music slipped through the tent, drums battling panpipes and fiddles wooing flutes. It was a relaxing sound at a distance. The breeze carried in the scent of burning herbs and the sea, and while it was pleasant, it set Bub to shivering.

I wrapped a blanket around him and went back to the table to grab one of the platters of food. Then we nestled into the pillows and ate some more, quietly enjoying the small stretch of peace we'd been granted.

As the fires died down outside, the tent grew dim, and even though I'd asked Bub not to think on our looming troubles, he whispered his worries to me in the dark.

"That soul, it was the one you harvested for Grim last year?" he asked, resting his chin on top of my head as he pulled me closer.

"Yes."

"Then the rebels have everything they need, and there's nothing to be done."

"No." If we were goners anyway, I didn't see any reason to hide the truth from him. "He's not the soul the rebels are after."

Bub tensed. "They seem to think so. How can you be so certain?"

"Because the soul they're after has been missing since Monday morning. I tried to find her, but I couldn't. So even if the rebels don't have her, everything is fucked. That's why we're supposed to be enjoying tonight," I said with a strained smile.

"I don't think all is lost. Not yet anyway."

"You don't understand. That soul is responsible for distributing the soul matter after the ball. When she doesn't, when it applies itself randomly and ends up blurring the borders of the afterlives, all hell is going to break loose. The rebels will have their war, one way or another."

"Yes," Bub whispered, "but a war we can fight. What they had planned would have been much worse. Seth would have seen the Witch of Endor take the place of Grim's soul."

"The Witch of Endor? Is that the reason for the backward Es?"

Bub snorted. "She's painfully clever, isn't she? To hear her go on and on about her stint in the eighth circle of Hell, her head twisted around, it's exhausting."

"So I've heard. She's in Grim's custody."

He shrugged. "Not for long."

"I don't see her escaping the floor of horrors on her own. She's shackled to a table."

"Who said anything about on her own? She has the Seal of Solomon. Demons can't help but do her bidding. Even I felt swayed in her presence. Seth used her to question me." He shivered and burrowed deeper into the pillows. "That's how they learned of our last meeting—though I had no idea you left your blood in the cave." He shot a curious glance down at me, and I blushed.

"It was silly. I just wanted to remember the night."

"How could you forget it? It was dreadful. My poor heart still hasn't recovered from that look you gave me."

I kissed his shoulder. "You deserved it for not telling me what you were doing right away."

"I suppose," he sighed. "Regardless, I'm of no use to the scoundrels now."

I nodded. "And without the throne soul and their demon puppeteer witch, they're not going to have much of a party tomorrow."

Bub twisted to look down at me again. "The witch will still make an appearance, I assure you."

"Grim has the ring. No voodooed demons are coming to her rescue."

"She doesn't need a ring to summon another soul. She's also a necromancer, and a rather powerful one at that. Why do you think Seth wants to put her on Grim's little throne?"

I was quiet for a moment, pondering the ball's surprise guest appearance. "It doesn't matter now. Neither of us can show our faces in Limbo City anyway. Let them deal with it on their own."

"I'm not exactly battle-worthy." Bub's breath slowed into a heavy, soothing rhythm, lifting my head with each inhale. I closed my eyes, feeling his warmth soak through me, and was soon lulled to sleep.

CHAPTER TWENTY-NINE

*"Love seeketh not itself to please, nor for itself hath any care,
but for another gives its ease, and builds a Heaven
in Hell's despair."*
—William Blake

The silver-gowned faerie was true to her word, waking us in the wee hours. I almost wondered if being captives of the fey would be worth going back to sleep for another hour or two. We stumbled around the tent, groping in the dark for our meager possessions. I helped Bub into my black robe and pulled my lace-less boots on before slinging the strap of my bag across my chest.

A heavy mist circled the isle, glowing softly around the smoldering embers along the beach. It was the only sign anyone had been there the night before. The fey and all of their instruments and tables of food were gone, leaving an empty stretch of sand under a hint of purple touching the horizon, morning whispering to a sleepy sky.

Bub limped across the beach beside me, determined not to rely on my shoulders. The silver twig was still fastened around his neck. Una waited near our boat. She held out her hand after we had climbed aboard.

"The necklace, please," she said, waiting patiently as Bub untied the knot in the cord.

As he placed it on her open palm, the island began to tremble. Two fey, the same ones who had delivered the bath, gave the boat a shove, driving it into the sea. The queen made her strange clicking noise again, and unseen beings maneuvered us back toward the opposite shore.

I didn't know where to go from here. Nowhere was especially safe. The mortal realm could provide a little cover, but their spoils were of no use to us beings of Eternity. Our only hope was that Grim was too busy fussing over the ball to spare a few guards to stake out my ship. If we could make it to my cabin undetected, we could spend the day in bed, enjoying each other's company a few hours more before the world crumbled around us.

The boat scraped the rocky shore on the edge of Summerland. I decided to leave it there. Bringing it back to the harbor would draw attention. I pulled the coin dial and shoved it into my bag, then tangled my fingers with Bub's before flipping a coin back to the harbor.

The dock was quiet this early in the morning. I didn't see the nephilim on the neighboring boat, but there was a pair at the harbor entrance. We crept up the ramp to my ship before they could spot us.

The bottom lock on my cabin door was busted, probably Abe's doing, but at least the deadbolt was still functional. Bub hobbled over to plop down on the edge of the bed, while I checked the windows and the French doors, pulling the curtains more tightly closed as I went.

When I was done checking over the room, I dug through the closet to find us some fresh clothes. I came up with a pair of sweats that would have never fit Bub before, but they worked just fine for him as he was now. He didn't bother with a shirt. The cuts and sores on his chest were beginning to heal, and he had a hard time leaving them alone, constantly scratching and picking. I found some salve in the bathroom and tossed it onto the bed before I changed into a fresh pair of jeans and a clean shirt.

The sky outside grew brighter and brighter, spilling past the curtains and lighting up the cabin. It was almost blinding in its quest to seek out every corner, reflecting off all the white fabric and shiny wood.

Bub squinted as he watched me apply the salve to his chest with my fingers, covering every inch until he glistened in the hard light. The sound of excited voices and boats docking outside had us holding our breaths. Guests attending the ball would be arriving most of the day. We hardly spoke for fear of someone hearing us.

Instead, we curled up under the white comforter on the bed and held each other. I couldn't sleep. Every noise sent my heart on a mission to self-destruct, and just as soon as I talked it down, something would set it off again.

Bub was like a deaf kitten, snoring soundly beside me. My hand rested against his shoulder, a safe distance from the worst of the damage on his chest. I was content to watch him sleep until sweat prickled along his brow, and he began to burn with fever. He tossed the covers back and groaned,

loudly enough that I felt the need to wake him before someone else did.

"Something's not right," I whispered as his eyes fluttered
open. "You're on fire. I should take a look at your leg. We
need to clean it at the very least."

Bub's brow creased. "I don't know if that's such a good
idea, love. Someone is sure to hear." The fey had politely ignored his screams of agony the night before, but there was no
way they would go unnoticed at the harbor.

"We have to do something." I chewed my bottom lip and
stood to pace the room, pausing at the desk.

The note and coin I'd left were gone, but my cellphone
was still tucked inside the top drawer. I thought of Maalik and
my suspicions. One look at Bub's trembling leg and I didn't
care. I flipped open the phone and called the only person I
knew could help us.

"Lady Meng's Teahouse, how may I be of service?" Jack
answered cheerfully.

"I need you to meet me at the ship, alone, with some of
Meng's best as soon as possible."

"Lana? Is that you?" Jack whispered. "The Guard has
been nosing around asking questions—"

"I'll explain everything when you get here. Please hurry,"
I said, hanging up without another word.

Bub moaned. He had dozed off again, his skin growing
brighter with fever. I slipped out of the cabin and snuck down
the back stairs to the kitchen, rummaging around the cabinets
until I found a bottle of vodka, a stack of hand towels, and a
first-aid kit with sutures. If Jack showed, he might actually

know what to do with all of this crap. If he didn't, well, a cocktail couldn't hurt.

I also snagged a couple of cans of soup and a box of crackers out of the pantry, along with a pair of spoons. My hands were already overflowing, but I managed to tuck a bottle of water under each arm, too.

Bub was twisted in the covers when I slipped back into the room. His teeth chattered loudly as he clawed his chest. I dumped everything on the desk and found the first-aid kit, digging out a packet of painkillers. I tore it open and dropped the pills into my hand, bringing them to the bed with one of the bottles of water.

"Hey." I shook Bub's shoulder until he squinted up at me. His eyes were glazed over, but he noticed the pills, and his mouth opened enough for me to drop them in. I lifted his head and tilted the bottle of water to his lips.

The sound of footsteps on the deck made me jump, and I ended up spilling water down the side of Bub's face. He didn't seem to notice. I recapped the bottle and tiptoed to the door, poking my head out to glance down the hallway.

Jack stood on the main deck, a drink carrier held out in front of him and an uncertain frown pinching his face. I waved my hand and whispered his name under my breath, drawing his attention. He hurried down the hall, glancing nervously over his shoulder.

Once we were closed inside the cabin, I took the tea from him and stepped back so he could see Bub sprawled on the bed. "He was working as a spy for Cindy. She wouldn't let him tell anyone," I blurted, watching a wrathful look screw up Jack's features. With his horns, the effect was chilling.

"Why didn't he just say so?" the demon spat.

"It's Cindy's fault. I'm completely okay with blaming it all on her," I said, setting the box of tea on a bedside table.

I tried to pull Bub into a seated position, but he was entirely unhelpful. I didn't hold it against him. I could feel his heart punching behind his ribcage, and his breath rushed out in a ragged struggle I was sure he'd lose if we didn't do something soon.

I gave Jack a pleading look. "Please, help me."

His frown didn't go anywhere, but he circled the bed and took Bub's other arm, working with me to lift him up against the headboard. I grabbed one of the cups of tea and slowly poured a small drink into his mouth. He coughed, choking on the bitter liquid.

"It's the good stuff," Jack said with a shrug as if anything good was expected to be difficult. Some days, it sure felt that way.

After gagging down half a cup, Bub's trembling finally subsided, and his fever dropped off. We lowered him back to the bed, and I wet one of the hand towels to wipe the dried sweat from his face.

"I have vodka and sutures. Do you think you could stitch up Bub's leg?" I asked.

Jack shook his head. "The tea will help with the infection, but I cannot in good conscience associate myself further." He sat at the desk chair, watching me with a bewildered expression. "You've known all along, haven't you?"

I couldn't bring myself to answer.

"Why would you keep that from me? Why would *he* keep that from me? Am I not trustworthy?"

"Of course you are." I sighed and sat on the edge of the bed. "And I haven't known all along. I didn't find out until after Josie died."

Jack didn't look much happier. "I stole tea from Lady Meng. She offered me her hospitality, opened her home and heart to me, and I've betrayed her."

"I'm sure she'd understand, given the circumstance," I said, dabbing the wet towel over Bub's chest. "But wait to tell her. Enjoy the ball first. It could very well be the last one."

Jack's sharp inhale made me second-guess my new honesty policy. "Is the war really so close at hand?"

"I'm afraid so," I said. "Make the most of it. Who knows where we'll be tomorrow."

Jack left in a hurry, hardly sparing Bub another look. He was still clearly upset by the deception, but also, I think his priorities had shifted. Meng was his new master. And not only that, but she treated him as an equal, and as a worthy companion. It was a new concept for Jack. He deserved to spend his final hours with Meng, and I wanted Bub to myself anyway.

The day slipped by too quickly, even with so little to do. I spent most of it lying next to Bub, feeding him crackers and tea whenever he stirred. I knew we would have to redress his leg eventually, but I was hoping Meng's mojo was at least doing him some good until we could coin off somewhere Bub's demonic screams wouldn't draw an audience.

The quiet moments in the cabin seemed to draw out my remorse, and I wondered where and how Winston was faring. I'd promised him twenty-four hours, but it seemed like an awfully long time to be at the mercy of the rebels. Surely, he had found Naledi by now, if she were even being held captive by them. I planned to coin off to Hell long enough to use a payphone to contact Maalik and let him know, seeing as how he had relieved me of the tracking device. It also seemed like a good way to keep him distracted from bothering Bub and me.

As the daylight began to fade, muting the glow inside the cabin, Bub finally woke long enough to have a more substantial meal and a lengthier conversation.

"I'm sorry this is the best I could find in the ship," I said, handing him a can of soup and a spoon.

He peeled the lid back and drank eagerly from the rim, forgetting the spoon entirely. I gave him my can of soup next, deciding I could wait. He needed nourishment far more than I did. When he finished, he gulped down a bottle of water.

"We have vodka and half a bag of crackers left in case you'd like dessert," I said.

Bub cringed softly. "The crackers are stale, though I didn't mind so much while forcing down that dreadful tea."

"You didn't seem to think it was all that bad when *I* was laid up at Meng's, and you came to visit."

"That was to impress you," he said with a grin. "Did it work?"

"Absolutely." I laughed and went to fetch a pair of plastic cups from the bathroom vanity.

The vodka bottle was dusty, having been forgotten below deck for a decade or better. I cracked it open and filled both cups halfway. Then Bub and I toasted to his health, our future, and various other lost causes.

"We could still come out on top," he said, looking bothered by my lack of hope. "You never know."

"We? You still consider us a part of Eternity's righteous brigade? Even though we're wanted fugitives?"

Bub nodded slowly. "I guess I do. I imagine Cindy has at least come clean to the council. How could she not, with the witch's message?"

"I don't think so." My heart ached for his optimism, but it was just too far out of reach. "They seemed to think it was a trick meant to motivate me into betrayal. Especially Grim, if you couldn't tell from the nephilim on the prowl. To my knowledge, Cindy was happy to let the council believe what they wanted."

Bub looked disheartened, but he kept trying. "Once the ball has passed, you'll see. Everything will be fine."

I sighed and stood to peek through the curtains over the French doors. The sky had faded to a dull gray, and a few lanterns on the far pier had already come on. The wind whistled, sounding lonely now that the voices and boats were quiet. Soon, the sound of a cherub quartet filtered through the windows, signaling the beginning of the ball.

In a few hours, Grim would arrive in the throne realm, and Winston wouldn't be there. We would have to be gone by then. Nowhere in the city would be safe, but I didn't have a clue where to go.

Before I could dwell too long on the dilemma, the cabin door groaned a splintering protest and then burst into flames. I ran to the bed, grabbed Bub around the middle, and pulled him off the far side. He grunted as his wrapped leg hit the floor, and then turned to cover me with his body when the cabin door exploded inside the room.

Chunks of flaming wood shot over our heads, landing on the desk and setting fire to the curtains. The bed shielded us from the worst of it, but it was ablaze, too. I crawled to the bathroom door and fumbled around beneath the sink until I came away with a fire extinguisher. Kevin had equipped every room with one after his little Latin mishap at the end of the summer.

I stormed back into the cabin, spraying the foam at the desk and outer wall first so it wouldn't damage the hull of the ship. Then I covered the bed before finally reaching the doorway, where Maalik hovered in all his glorious wrath, his wings flapping loudly in the small space. I had the urge to shoot foam in his face, but I refrained.

"Was that necessary?" I snapped, coming around the bed with the extinguisher nozzle raised.

"You've condemned us all." Maalik's voice filled the room and pierced my heart with panic. His eyes migrated to the other side of the bed, where Bub was struggling to pull himself off the floor. "For a traitor," he hissed. Smoke swirled in his pupils, but I took a step back, putting myself in his path.

"He was spying for Cindy. And I haven't condemned anyone. The rebels don't have Naledi," I said, directing his wrath back to me.

"You dare speak her name in front of the heathen?"

"Watch it, pal." I pointed the nozzle at his face. "I've got big news for you, but I'll gladly keep it to myself if you can't play nice."

It took longer than I expected, but the storm in Maalik's eyes finally passed, and his feet touched the floor. His wings slowed their agitated flapping and folded against his back, but the hard edges of his face could not be swayed.

"Speak your piece, and then we'll discuss your surrender to the council."

I gave him a contemptuous glare. "Well, now there's some motivation. You really know how to compel a confession, don't you?"

"Just get on with it," he said through gritted teeth.

I huffed and tossed the extinguisher on the bed. "Fine. Winston has a bracelet. Maybe you'll have better luck tracking him than Naledi. He's with the rebels. It was his idea to make the exchange," I added, watching Maalik's eyes swirl with smoke. "He thought he might be able to find Naledi that way."

Maalik's hand shot into the pocket of his robe. He pulled out the tracking device and twisted it around like he'd done it a thousand times since I showed him how. It beeped sporadically, and the angel's brows knit together as he watched the surface. "The coordinates are changing too quickly, and they're unfamiliar. I think the bracelets are useless," he concluded, giving me a pained look.

I stepped closer and glanced down at the compact. "Those are coordinates for the Sea of Eternity," I said. "And they're moving this way."

"The rebels must still think he is the soul in charge," Bub said, pulling himself up into the desk chair. One of the plastic cups was partially melted, but he tilted it back anyway, finishing off the splash of vodka left in the bottom. "They're going to attempt to sacrifice him and put the Witch of Endor on the throne at the ball."

"What?" Maalik whispered, his wide eyes shifting between Bub and me.

"The soul Grim has on the thirty-seventh floor, the one who can summon demons," I explained.

"We have to stop them." Maalik looked down at the compact again. "How long before they arrive?" he asked me.

The coordinates were moving fast. "Ten minutes at best," I said, hugging myself as a stiff wind funneled down the hallway and into the cabin. "Even if you do manage to stop the rebels, without Naledi, Eternity is lost."

Maalik frowned as his dark eyes lifted to my face. "You've given up before the battle has even begun."

"I don't know how much help I'll be strapped to a table in Grim's torture chamber." I gave him a tight smile. "You know that's where I'll end up if I show my face at the ball."

He sighed and shoved the compact back into his pocket. "I would never let that happen. You should know that by now."

The ship rocked suddenly, and we all reached for something to cling to as we were tossed about. The French doors flung open, smacking into the cabin walls and shattering glass across the floor. The wind ripped at the curtains and our hair, bringing with it a howling siren song in the distance. Bub and Maalik both closed their eyes and shuddered at the hypnotic cries whispering over the sea.

"I will kill the witch," Maalik said with a start. He backed out of the room, casting a sidelong glance at the churning sea through the open French doors. "The rebels will have no direction without her."

"The Seal of Solomon," I said before he could take off down the hall. "Keep the ring away from her. She's going to be difficult enough to face as a necromancer."

Maalik nodded and was gone, vanishing from the charred doorway.

The ship rocked again, and Bub hissed as his leg slammed against the desk. I hunched over and grabbed the bed as it started to slide away from the wall.

"We can't stay here," I shouted over the wind.

Bub kept one white-knuckled hand on the edge of the desk and reached his other out to me. I grabbed it and pulled him onto the bed. The wind pushed the blankets up against the wall, and the siren song grew louder.

Outside, the sea crested in the distance. A golden throne sparkled in the pale evening light, and on it sat Eurynome, the mermaid goddess Seth had recruited to increase his hold on the seas in Eternity and the mortal realm.

Bub closed his eyes again, the weight of the song pulling at him as it grew louder. I had hoped we would have more time, but it was a familiar wish, one I always longed for in his company. The boat crashed against the dock, sending us to the floor. I crawled over to the desk and grabbed my bag, banging my head against the wall as the sea shook us like a snow globe.

Winston's coin was warm in my trembling hand. It would be safe for now. Though not for very long. Still, we couldn't stay on the ship with the sea pitching us about and the sirens pressing in on us.

I took Bub's hand and pressed a kiss to it before flipping the coin.

CHAPTER THIRTY

"Your life is the fruit of your own doing.
You have no one to blame but yourself."
—Joseph Campbell

The throne realm sucked us in like a vacuum. The scathing wind cut off so suddenly that my ears popped and I felt like gravity might release me to the bright sky.

"Where are we?" Bub asked, pushing himself up off the picture-perfect lawn.

"The throne realm." I stood and helped him up, and together, we made our way to the cottage.

Morgan and Father Ron answered the door, their faces scrunched with anxiety.

"*This* is the Lord of the Flies?" Father Ron sounded baffled.

"What were you expecting?" Bub asked, limping past him to sit on the couch.

Father Ron followed, his hands waving in the air. "I don't know, perhaps someone a bit more…demonic. Horns maybe?"

Bub shrugged. "I've had some work done."

The priest fell silent as if the idea of plastic surgeons in the afterlife was too absurd to acknowledge. I wondered if Bub was serious or just couldn't resist tormenting a believer.

"Poor Winston," Morgan sighed, slumping next to Bub on the sofa. She frowned and leaned closer to him, sniffing sharply. "You've been to Avalon!" she squealed.

"We needed somewhere safe to stay the night," I said, trying to calm her outrage. "Una was very accommodating."

"She allowed you on the isle? But how?"

"Easy." I lifted the stone necklace from under my shirt.

Morgan stood and stamped her foot at me. "I gave that to Winston."

"And he gave it to me. It would have ended up in rebel hands if he hadn't."

She folded her arms and tilted up her nose with a har-rumph before dropping back down to the couch.

Father Ron stood in the doorway of the kitchen, wringing his hands over his white robe. "Shouldn't you be out tracking Winston down?"

I sighed and looked at the floor. "Maalik has the tracking device. The rebels are on their way to the city with Winston now."

He frowned. "You're not working with the angel to help rescue the boy?"

"I told Maalik how to find Winston," I said, glancing over at Bub. "We're not exactly welcome in the city right now, and he's in no position to be doing battle."

"Yes, but you look healthy," the priest said. "Winston made your role in all of this quite clear. You're important to

the fate of Eternity. Shouldn't you be doing more than dally-
ing around here?"

I pressed my lips together, feeling my cheeks warm. It
wasn't all cowardice keeping me just outside the fire ring.
There was a fair amount of hopelessness and selfishness
mixed in there, too.

"I don't really want to spend my final hours waging war,
not when I can spend them with someone I love," I said, slipping my hand into Bub's. He gave it a squeeze and frowned.

"This is only the end if you want it to be, love," he said
softly as if the words pained him. I could tell he didn't want
me to leave, but he also knew I should.

I knelt down and wrapped my arms around him. He held
me tightly, even though his breath grew strained at the pressure on his wounds. I pulled away and kissed him, avoiding
the healing cuts in the corners of his mouth. Bub gasped as
my hand brushed a tender spot on his chest, and then he
laughed nervously.

"We'll do all of this properly once you've returned," he
said, touching my cheek as I looked away. "You *will* return."

I gave him a weak smile, trying not to spoil his hopeful
outlook. Then I pressed my lips to his hand one last time and
left the cottage.

I walked across the grass, breathing in the warmth and
turning my face up to the sunny sky. I didn't want to abandon
this for the darkness and danger of the city.

Could I really make a difference, or was this all for nothing? Was it really worth the glory to go down fighting? And
what good was glory after you were dead?

CHAPTER THIRTY-ONE

"Never was anything great achieved without danger."
—*Niccolo Machiavelli*

It took a moment to wrap my mind around the idea that I was back in the game. It was disorienting after having accepted defeat for so long. I needed a plan, and preferably one that wasn't too dumb and dangerous. No sense in dying before I had the chance to make some noise.

I left the throne realm for the darkness of the city, stepping out of the travel booth across from Holly House into the cold night. Crickets chirped as I hurried past the front gate and inside.

Charlie spotted me in the lobby, and his mouth fell open in alarm as if he had never crossed paths with a fugitive. I slipped into an open elevator before he could say anything, and turned to smile at him, pressing a finger over my lips. As the doors closed, I saw him reach for his desk phone.

I rushed inside the condo and shot down the hall, straight to my room. My axe was in the trunk at the foot of the bed, and I also needed different shoes. I kicked off my lace-less boots in the closet and grabbed an older pair, one of which Josie had rendered holey with an arrow. I stuffed a knife down in one after lacing them up. Then I shoved the coin dial into my pocket and ditched my bag.

Pounding at the condo door hurried me along as I snatched up my axe and strapped it across my back. Then I remembered Morgan's necklace and gave it a twist as I slipped down the hall. Keys jingled in the kitchen, and I stepped back out of the way as the front door was pushed open. Several nephilim guards fluttered into the condo, followed by Holly Spirit and Charlie.

"You're sure it was her?" Holly asked the deskman. He nodded gravely, looking right through me as he scanned the condo.

They stepped farther into the dining room, and I crept behind them, silently cursing myself for not waiting to put on the boots. The soles squeaked ever so lightly on the hardwood, but it was enough to turn Holly's head.

Her hand reached out, swiping through the air and grazing the edge of my axe. She pulled away with a sharp inhale and clutched her fingers. "Here!" she shouted, drawing the guards out of the bedrooms they were raiding and back into the kitchen.

I stumbled out through the front door and ran down the carpeted hallway to the elevators, turning a desperate circle after I'd slapped the button. The guards were too close. I'd never make it in time. Holly's blood dripped from the corner of my axe and dotted the carpet, giving away my location. Thinking fast, I fumbled through my pocket to find the throne coin and flipped it into the air.

The sunny cottage scene was like a painting, but I didn't stay to enjoy it, quickly flipping the coin again to find myself in the lit travel booth outside Holly House, the only spot the coin was spelled to access in the city. I stayed in the booth and dropped a regular coin into the slot, taking it to the harbor and quickly exiting before someone notified the guards watching the entrance about my invisible trickery.

The quick succession of realm jumping made my head spin, and I stumbled as I raced down the dock and up the ramp to my ship. The sea still rocked violently as if someone had pulled the drain and the soulish water was being stirred and sucked into a typhoon around the city. I squatted low on the deck, trying to hold my ground as the ship cracked into the dock. The piers groaned and wobbled.

I couldn't see Eurynome and her fishy followers now that night had fallen, and the lanterns glared across the dock, but I knew they had to be close. Their eerie song spurred on the storm, wailing in time with the thrashing waters.

I hurried over to the ship's main mast and pulled the coin dial out of my bag, inserting it back into the dash of Warren's bike. Between the turbulence and my shaking hands, it was impossible to untie it from the mast. I finally gave up and used my axe to slice through the rope.

The dock creaked again, and I heard something break loose in the distance. A post ripped from the far pier as a barge was carried away by the waves. And then the dock lanterns went out. I blinked, adjusting to the darkness until the faint light at the horizon illuminated the sea. It was alive, and it was angry.

I held my breath as I watched the water pull away from the seawall surrounding the city, leaving a naked, sooty floor behind. Mossy pillars stretched beneath the dock, disappearing into the shadows below. The surf reeled back as if winding up for a knockout blow and rushed at the city.

I fired up the bike, dumped the clutch, and barely touched the ramp as I abandoned ship, flying down the dock toward the entrance. The two nephilim standing guard tried to flag me down, then noticed the sea on my tail and took flight, heading inland.

I couldn't hear the sirens anymore, but their song had been replaced by another. The sea wailed, crying out like a stampede of lost souls. In my side view mirror, I saw their ghostly, twisted faces with empty eyes and gnashing teeth. Their fingers broke the surface of the wave's peak, grasping and flailing at nothing until the wave crashed across Market Street.

The watery souls clung to the street and buildings, pulling themselves forward as they grew more solid. The sea rose and fell again, bringing more souls with it. They too crawled their way out of the water, their pale flesh glowing against the blackout darkness of the city.

My skin crawled and broke out in a cold sweat as I sped down Morte Avenue, fleeing the nightmare. Lightning splintered through the sky, quickly followed by rain. The weather was spelled in Limbo, and precipitation was rarely part of the forecast for this part of the island, and certainly never allowed on the night of the ball.

Up ahead, the beam from my headlight fell over Athena's dummy guards, lined up on the sidewalk out front. I blasted my horn as I passed, trying to give them a warning before the zombified ghosts of the sea swarmed the boutique.

I cut up Destiny Avenue, and my tires squealed as I turned left onto Council Street. Reapers Inc. was just a block away. I could see the glowing light of lanterns anchored around the roof. Of course Grim would have a backup generator.

The moan of souls echoed all around me, and I saw them creeping in off the north side of the island, too. Rain ran in rivers along the gutters and puddled in the street. The sound of it filled my head and clouded my thoughts, and the cold sharpness of it beat my face and arms. I could barely feel my fingers.

Through the front window of Reapers Inc. I saw a dozen nephilim guards standing watch in the lobby, their feathers ruffled and twitchy as they watched the storm building outside. Ball attendees clustered behind them, their fancy gowns soaked, and their elaborate hairdos ruined. A few of the more done up ladies dabbed at streaky makeup.

I stashed the bike behind the front bushes and twisted Morgan's necklace again. I didn't have time for stalling with the guards. They would all be up soon enough once the souls came into view.

The wind prodded at the front doors, rattling them against their frames. When I pushed one open and slipped inside, no one paid any attention. I didn't have to try my luck at the elevators. One opened as I neared, and a handful of pouty goddesses sulked out into the lobby. I took their place and pressed the button for the roof.

The few minutes of quiet solitude didn't bring much relief. I puzzled over what I would do once I reached the top. I had no idea what the rebels' next move would be. I thought of the witch and her ring and wondered if Maalik had accomplished what he'd set out to do. Just to be sure, I pressed the button for the thirty-seventh floor. The car screeched to a halt at the last second.

The overhead lights in the faux office were out, but the storm outside filled the room with lightning. The smears of blood on the floor hadn't been cleaned up, so I used them to find my way back to the soul's room, only pausing when the darkness settled around me until the storm lit the path again.

My wet boots squished softly on the floor, and my breath grew labored as my heart beat out a warning that became more and more difficult to ignore. Something fluttered nearby as I twisted through the maze of plastic sheeting. It sounded like a bird trapped in an oil slick.

A burst of lightning filtering through the layers, and I glanced down to make sure I was still on the right trail. The blood looked brighter, fresher. I looked up as the light dissipated, seeing the plastic in front of me for a split second. I stepped forward, squinting through the dark.

The lightning came again, sharper and more vibrant. It illuminated the plastic, caked with dark blood. I yelped as a hand slapped and streaked through the carnage, and the flapping noise came again. The hand gripped the plastic and ripped it from the ceiling.

Maalik lay on the other side in a puddle of blood. His eyes rolled up to me, and he croaked out a rasping, wet breath. The lightning slipped away as I dropped my axe and knelt beside him, my open hands trembling uselessly.

"What can I do?" I whispered, feeling for him in the dark. Tears burned my eyes, and I choked out a terrified sob as I waited for another streak of light to guide me.

When it came, Maalik latched on to my hand and directed it down his body. The handle of something stuck out through a hole in his robe, pinning the fabric to his side. I pulled the garment away and ripped it open, exposing his bloody skin beneath.

"Take it out," he said stiffly, choking on his own blood. I hesitated, and he found my hand again, squeezing it so hard I thought it might break. "Take. It. Out."

I grabbed the handle and jerked it free. It was a serrated blade of some sort, probably from Grim's cart of interrogation tools. Maalik groaned and collapsed onto his opposite side, folding his wings back to keep from crushing them. His fingers twitched as they probed his injury, and the smell of burning flesh made me gag. He was cauterizing his own wound with hellfire.

When he finished, he sat up and shook out his wings. Blood speckled the floor and my arms. It dripped from the ends of Maalik's feathers, staining them a dusty pink. He pulled off the ruined robe and dropped it to the floor as he stood. The waistband of his dress pants was soaked with blood, too.

"The witch?" I asked, shaking as he helped me to my feet.

Maalik nodded. "She has the ring. She summoned a demon to distract me as she escaped."

"We need to get to the roof," I said, picking up my axe. "There's something you should see."

We hurried back through the plastic maze to the elevator. The building grumbled as we rode up, and the backup lights in the car flickered. Taking the stairs would have been the smart thing to do, but running nearly forty flights wouldn't leave much stamina for a battle. Not for me anyway.

Maalik examined the angry red mark along his ribcage in the mirror spanning the back wall of the elevator. "I never imagined an original believer would take to the rebels willingly. Their resourcefulness grows more tiresome each day it seems."

"You have no idea," I said under my breath as we stepped out onto the roof. The rain drenched us instantly.

Most of the guests had gone inside to seek shelter, but a few huddled under the cover of several gazebos scattered around the outside of the dance floor. A dozen guards stood watch too, but they were too distracted to notice us.

I gripped the stone ledge enclosing the rooftop and gazed out over the city. The souls from the sea had reached the building, and they were climbing up the side like giant, ghostly spiders. It reminded me of the way the demons had clung to the building under the summon of the witch.

Maalik was speechless. He watched the souls approach with wide eyes, his hand clasped over his mouth in shock.

I turned, peering out across the roof, taking in each face until I found her. She was sitting at a table by herself. The rain almost concealed her presence, but those haunting eyes glowed in the dark. She saw me too, and her face lit with an eerie smile.

"There," I said softly to Maalik.

He turned around, and the soul's smile darkened. Fear flickered across her face, and her hands reached out to grab the chair in front of her, lifting it in time to fend off the blast of hellfire Maalik sent spiraling across the empty dance floor.

The guards took flight, circling the roof like spooked pigeons until they zeroed in on the commotion. Maalik pointed after the witch.

"Seize her!" he shouted. "She wields the seal again."

The nephilim swooped after the witch, trying to box her in with their spears, but there wasn't enough time. The first of the souls reached the rooftop. The remaining guests watched them a moment, confused and shocked by their presence. Then two of the crazed souls tackled a guard and began chewing on his wings.

The roof erupted in screams as everyone rushed for the elevators. The angels and beings that could fly hovered out of the souls' reach. Some lifted other guests up with them, fleeing the scene. The building shook violently as if an earthquake were trying to shrug the tiny island right off the face of Eternity. Shrieks echoed into the night as the possessed souls continued to flood the rooftop, crawling over the dance floor like fire ants.

Maalik and I climbed on top of the stage at the far end of the roof. I slung my axe off my shoulder and nudged a soul back as it tried to follow. Another bumped into him, and together they ambled off, oblivious under the witch's spell.

When the elevators returned for a second lot of guests, more nephilim guards stepped out onto the roof. They pointed their spears at the souls, herding them back away from the elevators as the lesser deities made their escape.

The souls crowded each other, swaying like the waves they'd come from until they were shoved forward by the growing masses, impaling each other on the guards' spears. It seemed profane to harm them, knowing all they did was at the command of the witch. They had no control.

I scanned the roof again and found her squatting atop a gazebo. Her wild eyes pulsed, and I saw the signal reflected in the vacant eyes of the souls. Their onslaught grew fiercer and more determined.

A deep, bellowing horn sounded in the distance. Over the churning sea past the northern edge of the island, lightning grazed a battleship bearing the mark of the demon Amy, Gabriel's ex-lover and Xaphen's daughter. She commanded thirty-six legions, and it looked as if she'd brought every last one of them.

A swarm of winged demons took flight off the deck of the ship. Gabriel was with them. They carried axes and bows, swinging them threateningly as they darted through the rain and dodged bolts of lightning.

The witch watched with a hungry grin crinkling her face. One hand gripped the edge of the gazebo's roof. The other, displaying the Seal of Solomon, danced through the rain, and I realized everything was about to go horribly wrong.

CHAPTER THIRTY-TWO

*"Ultimately we know deeply that
the other side of every fear is freedom."*
—*Marilyn Ferguson*

Amy's demons lined the roof, shoulder to shoulder behind the mass of souls. Their eyes burned in time with the Witch of Endor's, and their weapons pointed at the small crowd gathered in the center of the dance floor. They had infiltrated the building and brought Grim and the other council members they found to stand among us to await judgment.

The boss man gave me a dark look, the kind that made me think it would be a mercy not to survive this. I steered clear of him, choosing instead to hide in Maalik's shadow. Cindy Morningstar stood with the council too, though there was a tightness to her eyes as if she were battling against the pull of the witch's ring.

Parvati, the Hindu goddess on the council, looked torn, too. She held the power to transform into Kali, the goddess of destruction, and she could have made short work of the slew of demons on the roof if she wanted. The fact that they were on *our* side and momentarily possessed seemed to weigh on her conscience, and destroying our own armies would only benefit the rebels in the end.

Gabriel wasn't among the winged demons or the hostages, and my heart reeled at the possibility of him being badly hurt or dead. I looked around the roof, trying to make out any other familiar faces. Meng Po and Jack were missing. So was Horus. But I was most surprised not to see Jenni. The elevators had been blocked off, and I imagined the building sheltered hundreds more hostages on its many floors.

The rain eased up, fading into a sprinkle, and the rushing noise was replaced by a slow and steady *whoosh, whoosh, whoosh.* The crowd looked up as a chariot descended on us. It hung from a giant wheel lined with oars, like a bastardized version of a helicopter, and it was run by a withered old man in a bird mask, most likely another recruit from Summerland.

Seth loomed behind the odd pilot, his elbow reclined over one side of the chariot. The rebel god hadn't made an appearance since he was exposed as a traitor on the council, and though it had only been a year, he looked much older. His face was lined like tree bark, and his red eyes burned fiercer than ever. Winston stood next to him. The kid was still as death and unblinking, clearly under the witch's spell. It unnerved me that I couldn't reach him.

A harpy dove down to the roof to scoop up the witch, delivering her to the chariot on the opposite side of Winston. The rebel duo hovered there a moment, gloating in victorious elation. Then Seth passed the witch a dagger. She placed her hand on top of Winston's head, craning it back until he looked up at the sky.

As I watched in horror, the witch pulled the blade across his throat. It all happened so fast, there was nothing to be done. Winston slumped over the side of the chariot, his blood spilling in a thick stream from his neck into the shadows of the city below.

Grim's outrage echoed out in a thunderous battle cry. The crowd parted with a gasp as his black eyes met Seth's, sending a sliver of panic through the old god's expression. I took a stab in the dark and decided that Maalik hadn't found time to tell Grim that Winston was no longer the throne soul. Either that, or he just didn't want to be the unlucky messenger.

Grim tore off his robe. The scars along his back spasmed, and I knew what came next. I'd seen his nightmarish show before. Bones snapped, and flesh ripped as his black wings freed themselves from the cocoon of his body. Even uncertain, Seth looked smug as if forcing Grim's transformation had been his intent.

"Behold," Seth shouted from his chariot. "The Greek god Thanatos. How can he claim to be a neutral party to the council when he hails from an afterlife himself?"

Grim was silent, flapping his wings stiffly to flick away the blood and meaty bits clinging to them. His dark eyes took in Seth like a hawk eyeing its prey.

"What say you to that, Thanatos?" Seth said, trying to force a reply. "Or did your little soul here grant your voice as well as your power over Eternity?" He grabbed the back of Winston's robe and chucked his body over the side of the chariot.

I sucked in a shaky breath and blinked back my tears. Maalik's hand found mine. He pulled me in closer and took a quick glance around. "Do you have your throne coin?" he whispered. I gave him a short nod. "Then use it."

"No. I didn't come all the way up here to bail now."

Seth scanned the crowd, his eyes lit on Maalik and me, but he continued on, searching for someone else. "Ah, here she comes. Finally."

Jack and Lady Meng stepped off the elevator and slipped through the crowd. Meng carried a tray of tea. She hesitated at the edge of the dance floor, and Jack prodded her forward, the witch's glow filling his eyes.

I was furious, but I knew the second I made a move, all hell would break loose. Grim would kill me the first chance he got, but I was still somehow waiting for his signal. Old habits die hard, I guess.

As Jack escorted Meng up to the edge of the roof, the harpy swooped down again to take the tray from her. I had a moment of panic, wondering if the tea might actually accomplish something if Naledi *were* dead.

The witch fingered through the various cups. She downed the first one, cringing and shaking her head as if the concoction were spoiled milk mixed with moonshine. I guess the eighth circle of Hell was limited to contortionism. She blinked a few times and smacked her lips.

"Well?" Seth demanded.

She held up a finger. "I think I feel something. Yes, something is definitely happening."

The wheel above the chariot made a crackling noise. A stick of some sort plunged through a gap in the spokes, and several splintered as they snapped and broke away from the wheel. The bird-masked man grasped for the culprit, but they vanished as quickly as they had appeared.

The chariot tilted on its side, struggling to hold its place in the sky. The witch held on to the tea tray, cradling it as she tried to lift another cup to her lips, while Seth slugged the man in the bird mask.

"What was that?" he growled.

The man twisted the rod holding up the wheel and waved Seth away. The chariot steadied and then tilted to the other side before finally crashing onto the corner of the roof. Everyone scrambled back and out of the way as the contraption choked out its final breath.

Grim was on Seth a second later, snatching the old god as he threw one leg over the side of the broken chariot. The possessed demons trained their bows on him, but he was unmoved.

"Your intentions are to kill me anyway, so why shouldn't I have the satisfaction of ripping out your throat first?" Grim snapped in Seth's face.

Four souls crept in behind him, but Grim took flight, taking Seth with him, his hands grasped around the god's neck. He hovered just beyond the building, dangling Seth over the seventy-five-story drop to the street below.

"Go ahead," Grim said to the witch. "Set your minions on me and see what happens to your precious leader."

The witch smiled. "He's not my leader. *I* am his, and he is expendable."

Seth looked just as surprised as Grim as the witch nodded to the demons. Arrows rained down on the dueling gods, sticking in Grim's wings and body until he could take no more. He fell out of the sky, dragging Seth down with him, and they were swallowed up by the same darkness that had claimed Winston.

The crowd shrank away from the witch as she threw back another cup of tea, shaking her head afterward in a disturbingly elastic show, her chin nearly touching her spine. She stepped forward, enjoying the gasps of fear she provoked from those nearest.

"Any more questions?" she cooed, her eyes lighting with amusement as they fell on me.

"Just one," I said. My fingers itched for my axe, but the demons' arrows seemed to gravitate wherever the witch looked. Right now, that was at me. "How do you expect to take over the throne while another soul has claim to it?"

Her smile tensed. "I killed the soul who had claim to it. You delivered him yourself, remember?"

Whispers rippled up from the crowd, but I didn't let them distract me. Maalik still held my hand, and I pulled courage from his presence.

"I was told to deliver a soul of importance, not the throne soul."

The witch's glowing eyes narrowed, and her grin twisted into a snarl. "If that wasn't the throne soul, then where is it?"

"Here."

The end of a staff cracked against the side of the witch's head, sending her to the ground with a wounded cry. Naledi stepped up behind her, a twisted staff in hand. I recognized it as the same stick that had crippled the chariot.

The Egyptian girl wore a simple shift dress that fell to her knees. Her dark skin almost disappeared against the backdrop of the night, making her bluish aura all the brighter.

She was alive. She was here. Everything was forever changed, but something vaguely resembling a future began to form in the back of my mind.

Naledi stepped on the witch's wrist and reached down to yank the demon ring free. She held it up for the crowd, and then brushed her fingers together, crumbling it into nothing more than stray soul matter that dissipated in the air like dust.

The demons lining the roof sighed all at once, dropping their weapons and falling to the ground. They touched their arms and faces as if trying to confirm that they were truly in control of their own bodies again. Jack wept at Meng Po's feet, and she stroked her weathered hand across the space between his horns, trying to soothe him.

"Child," the witch snarled, wriggling beneath Naledi's bare foot. She strained away from the girl, her hands sprawling out to summon those she still held dominion over. "I'll have that throne yet."

The countless souls filling the roof jolted awake as light shot through their eyes. They ambled forward, mouths open and teeth scraping together, searching for the object of the witch's desire.

Naledi lifted the gnarled staff over her head. An intense blaze emanated from it, spreading out to encompass the roof. She waved it through the air, and the souls became boneless, sloshing to the ground like the water they had risen from.

They spilled over the edge and ran down the side of the building before rushing along the street and back into the sea.

The witch screamed and thrashed, slapping at Naledi's legs, but the girl didn't seem bothered at all. She bent down and pressed her hand to the witch's chest, and a familiar power spilled out of her, one I thought I only shared with Grim. The soul's eyes filled with panic as Naledi took hold of her insides and pulled her upright for all to see.

"For Winston," she said and ripped the witch's heart from her chest. I took a step back, startled that she'd chosen such a graphic end when she could have simply pulled the witch out of existence.

The shell of the soul collapsed into a lifeless heap as Naledi turned to address the crowd, the heart still in hand. Steam wisped around it, glowing against the chill of night.

"My name is Naledi, and I sit on the Throne of Eternity. If anyone else dares to take it from me, let them come forward now and try."

The rooftop was silent. She could have whispered the words and been heard by all. The members of the council shifted uncomfortably as if they wanted to protest and state their case for democracy, but the dripping heart in Naledi's hand seemed to give them pause.

"No one else here wants the throne," I said softly. "These are good people, and you're scaring them."

Naledi blinked at me, and then at the bleeding heart in her hand. "She brought this on herself," she called out to the crowd as if that would placate them.

"You should address the council privately," I said, trying to prompt her in the right direction.

Naledi dropped the heart and rubbed her hand down the front of her white dress, smearing it with blood. "Right. Councilors, please convene with me in the…" She looked to me for help.

"The conference room on the seventy-third floor is the usual spot."

Naledi nodded and tapped the staff on the ground. "Yes. That will do."

Everyone slowly began to move around and take inventory of each other. For a moment, it seemed like the worst of things was over. Naledi motioned for me to follow her to the elevators with the council. I was sure she had a million questions, and so did I.

I didn't expect to find my face slammed into the ground so soon after apparent victory.

"You will not get away with this." Grim's breath slid across my neck. His fingers dug into my shoulder as he rolled me onto my back, and then his hands were around my throat, squeezing until my air cut off.

His wings fell in long, hard strides, creating a wind that made my eyes water. An arrow was lodged in his back, the point stabbing through the front of his shoulder and coming dangerously close to my face. I counted four more, sticking out from his thighs and torso.

My adrenaline was having a hard time kicking into gear with the day I'd had, but as the world went spotty, I finally felt it tingle up through my arms. I placed one hand on the center of Grim's chest and waited for the heat to flow through me.

Something sliced over my head and hot blood sprayed my face as Grim let go, his hands going to his face with a scream.

My lungs filled with a deep breath and my eyes rolled up to find Jenni standing behind me, her katana pointed at Grim. Maalik hovered behind her, his wings snapping furiously as his eyes swirled with hellfire.

Blood trickled through Grim's fingers as he glared at them. "I'll remember this," he hissed, his wings struggling to lift him away from the roof. Several nephilim guards moved in around him, looking uncertain of whether they should assist or detain.

Grim snarled in their direction, sending them back a step, and then he dove off the side of the building, disappearing into the night.

Jenni sheathed her sword, but she didn't look overly happy with me. "Pretty sure I'm fired," she said, her nose curling up distastefully. "I don't even like you right now, but at least we're even."

"Thanks," I said, grunting as she helped me up.

"If he comes back for seconds, you're on your own."

"Fair enough."

Naledi called out to me impatiently from an elevator, as if I hadn't just narrowly escaped being strangled to death by my irate boss. I rubbed my neck and huffed out an incredulous sigh. The girl had a lot to learn. But so did all of Eternity.

CHAPTER THIRTY-THREE

*"What we have done for ourselves alone dies with us;
what we have done for others and the world
remains and is immortal."*
—*Albert Pike*

Autumn in Limbo City looked the same as always. It seemed odd with everything that had happened, that so much was still unchanged.

The tulip trees in the park crunched softly in the breeze, their bright leaves raining down as I drank my hot chocolate on Josie's marble memorial bench. I'd found Kevin here the morning after the fateful ball, shivering in his work robe, his hand pressed tenderly over the engraved message. Saul had watched over him all night, curled up under the bench. A spell over the park had kept the noise from the city at bay, and they'd completely missed the chaos.

Gabriel had missed it, too. I had found him in Amy's care. When the Witch of Endor took control of the demon's flying legions, they'd unwittingly mauled the angel, knocking him right out of the fight. Amy had sought him out and dragged him inside her father's bar to tend to his fractured wing and leg. He was banged up pretty badly, but he seemed to think it was all worthwhile, considering that he and Amy were talking again.

Naledi made quite an impression on the council. With Grim off the grid and his secret out in the open, it was hard telling when or if he would show his face again, so she had taken his seat as the neutral party on the council. Morgan and Father Ron served as her personal committee. They called themselves the Apparition Agency.

Naledi tried to put me in charge of Reapers Inc. in Grim's absence, but I promptly pointed her to Jenni, the official second-in-command. Naledi was resistant, and it took me admitting in front of the entire council that my math skills were lacking—and would result in an apocalypse all on their own—to convince her that it was a bad move. Jenni confirmed my shitty math theory and happily took the job, finally forgiving me for all the things I'd kept from her in fear of losing my head.

I confronted Cindy about Bub's secret mission, too. She tried to deny it at first, but when I threatened to call her out in front of the council, she chose to come clean on her own, clearing Bub's name so he could come out of hiding and reclaim his frozen accounts.

Cindy hadn't been the only one keeping secrets on the council. The *not so little* bird that had informed Morgan of my arrival turned out to be Horus's falcon. Naledi had consulted with the god on the troubling visions she had of the future, and he had agreed to help in any way he could. He had been across the sea in Nirvana, searching for another original believer, when the city came under attack.

Naledi's own absence had been spent in the mortal realm, tracking down the Staff of Moses. She had seen the demonic ring and the witch in her visions, and she knew the staff was the only thing that could thwart an army born of the sea, even if it wasn't a Red one.

Seth's body was never found, but the graffiti around the city stopped, so that was something. The rebels weren't kaput, but they were giving us a chance to catch our breath, and for that I was thankful.

"Are you ready?" Bub limped across the park, leaning heavily on a shiny cane. His leg was still healing, and it was in a proper cast now, but it was hidden nicely beneath a navy-blue suit today. Other than the cane, the only visible signs of his abuse were the faint scars at the corners of his mouth. They seemed to disappear entirely when he smiled at me.

I stood up from Josie's bench and finished my hot chocolate, tossing the paper cup into the trash bin at the park entrance as we left.

The wind was more biting away from the cover of the pretty trees, and I tightened my scarf around my neck before huddling in against Bub. I couldn't bring myself to wear jeans to the memorial, so I'd dug out a pleated skirt and matched it with a pair of tights and tall boots.

A small crowd waited for us at the end of the dock where the far pier had been repaired after the storm. Jenni and Kevin were in their work robes. They'd taken off early to attend. Maalik stood behind them. Naledi, Morgan, Father Ron, and Horus were there, too. A small bundle wrapped in white cloth lay before them.

"I wanted to bring him back to Duat," Horus said, his face shadowed with regret. "He would have been treated like a king."

"He was a king," Naledi said. It didn't seem to occur to her that kings rarely fetched things for others with the sort of vigor and admiration Winston had shown for her.

Naledi nodded to Horus, and he gently unfolded the cloth, revealing the gray body inside. Winston looked so small, like he had in the hospital where we'd first met. My throat tightened, and I swallowed back the lump trying to form there.

Horus cradled his body and slowly lowered it into the sea. Ghostly hands reached up to take Winston, pulling him gently along the currents until he disappeared beneath the waves. I sat on the edge of the dock and watched the tide wash in and out, wondering how long it would be before Winston's fractured soul would be sucked up by the Fates' Factory. The fragmented soul matter was just as recyclable, but he'd never be the same Winston we knew again.

Kevin and Jenni each touched a hand to my shoulder before walking back down the dock. Horus and Maalik left for subcommittee meetings, Morgan and Father Ron went back to the throne realm, and Bub went to wait on the ship. Naledi sat down on the pier next to me.

"Why didn't you let Winston in on your plan?" I asked.

She blinked at me, considering the question a long while before answering. "I loved Winston," she finally said, looking back out across the sea. "He was very good to me. The throne is not an easy thing to master, and he helped me understand the weight of it better than he realized."

"I don't get it," I said. "If Winston was so wise, it seems like you would have asked for his help."

Naledi sighed. "It's hard to explain. The throne reveals so much. It makes it tempting to change fate, but every changed outcome affects a dozen more." She gave me a sad look. "If I had let Winston tell you that Josie's death was foretold, can you tell me you wouldn't have tried to prevent it?"

"No. I would have absolutely prevented it." That was a no-brainer.

"Exactly," Naledi said. "But the universe demands balance. Her life would have only been spared in exchange for yours, and without you, the ball would have had a very different ending last week. Limbo City might not be here at all."

"I don't see how I played that big of a role, and that still doesn't explain why you left Winston out of the loop."

She took a deep, frustrated breath. "Are you glad to have your demon back?"

I smiled. "Yes. Very much so."

"If Winston had known I was safe, do you think he would have had the courage to exchange his life for your lover's?"

"You knew he would do that?" It seemed like such a brave act for Winston, but knowing Naledi had set it up made the whole thing stink, and I had gone along with it. What kind of friend did that make me?

A tear ran down Naledi's cheek. "The rebels have been stopped, for now, and Grim's stranglehold on the throne is broken. Your reunion with the demon was a coincidence, but it would not have been possible without Winston's sacrifice either."

She had given up the one person who loved her most, and even though I knew it hadn't been her intention, it still felt like she had done it for me so I could have Bub back.

"I'm sorry," I said softly, resting my hand on her shoulder.

We sat on the pier for a while longer until the sky began to darken, and then she coined back to the throne realm, and I headed to the ship.

The dock had done some damage to the hull during the storm, but the boat was still sailable. Luckily, Kevin was eager to get back to his remodeling duties. He seemed to have kicked his hellfire problem, but he stayed a couple of nights at Meng's for tea therapy anyway. Or maybe it was just to escape my and Bub's reign of passion over the condo. Jenni didn't seem to notice as much now that she practically lived at Reapers Inc.

Bub was still interviewing architects for the rebuild of the summer manor, and his flat in Pandemonium had already been rented out to another demon. He was basically homeless, though we were looking into buying a houseboat together.

As I entered my cabin, Bub looked up from the desk with a grin. "What do you think?" he asked, waving his hand around the room.

The bedding and curtains that Maalik had scorched were gone, replaced by dark, red silk. It made the room look like it was made for sinning in.

"I like it." I grinned and pulled off my scarf, draping it over the back of the chair. "What's that?" There was a scrap of paper on the desk. It looked like someone had folded and unfolded it about a zillion times.

Bub glanced down at it. "I found it at the park under Josie's bench. I thought maybe you'd dropped it…but I must confess. I took a peek. I believe you left it for your apprentice the night you came for me?"

I unfolded the note and smiled.

Bub chuckled as he read over my shoulder. "Your many titles are quite colorful. I especially like the last one."

Grasshopper,

It's been an honor being your mentor. I know I'm not what you expected or deserve, but I did my best. I hope you know that. There's something I have to do, and I don't expect to survive the night. I know you're battling enough demons as it is, but please don't fall apart over me. I'm at peace, and all that gooey spiritual crap I'm no good at putting into words. Let Jenni and Gabriel know that I love them, and I love you, too. All I ask is that you take care of yourself. I know that's what Josie would have wanted.

Captain Lana Harvey
of the O'Malley Ghost Ship
Esteemed Leader of the Posies
Slayer of Rebel Scum

P.S. Don't forget to feed Saul. Seriously, he'll eat your shoes. And it's three scoops, though four works on a bad day.

Catch up with Lana and company in…

GHOST MARKET

LANA HARVEY, REAPERS INC. BOOK SIX

Available Now in Print, eBook, and Audio!

Soul-searching is a dirty business.

In the wake of a thwarted war, Lana Harvey is more than ready for an extended vacation on the new houseboat she shares with the Lord of the Flies, but when the leaderless rebels begin poaching souls and selling them on the Ghost Market, Lana is tasked with heading up a new unit to stop them.

Having one of the most famous faces in Eternity proves challenging when it comes to finding a way inside the secretive world of illegal soul peddling, and the only person Lana knows with the right connections is Tasha Henry, a former colleague and defeated rebel with a poaching record. The rogue reaper isn't going to be easy to track down, and even if Lana does manage to catch up with her, the real question is whether or not a shot at redemption will be enough to lure her away from the dark side.

ACKNOWLEDGMENTS

2019 10-year anniversary update: I can hardly believe that Lana turns 10 this year! To celebrate, I asked Rebecca Frank to revamp the cover designs, my cousin Kaitlyn Beck to pose as Lana, my husband Paul to photograph her, and my editor Chelle Olson to clean up my early work that I heavily relied on English-savvy teacher pals to proofread back in the day. I also can't forget shout-outs to Hollie Jackson, the epic narrator who voices Lana in the audiobooks; the Four Horsemen of the Bookocalypse, my amazing critique group; and THE professor George Shelley, whose enthusiasm for Lana's world motivated me at times I'd almost given up on writing. All my gratitude to you wonderful mavens who make my books shine and my heart swell.

Original acknowledgments: This has been a very big year for me. I quit my graphic design day job and moved my family to the Lake of the Ozarks, where I'm now writing full-time. All thanks to you guys, my awesome readers! So many of you have emailed to let me know how much you've enjoyed my Lana books, or to ask when the next one will be out. It really makes my day, and I promise I'm typing just as fast as I can.

Special shout out to Bryony Curtis, who won the quote scramble game on the *Read'Em & Reap Blog Hop* last year. The prize was a soul cameo in this book, which took place in the circus scene of chapter one. I hope you all enjoyed it!

Of course, I can't forget to thank all of the wonderful peeps who continually offer their feedback and support, blasting typos and saving me from myself: my husband Paul with his magical lexicon; my critique group, the Four Horsemen of the Bookocalypse; and Professor George Shelley, to whom this book is dedicated. I'd be completely lost without you guys.

All remaining errors are my own…and probably intentional.

ABOUT THE AUTHOR

USA Today bestselling author **Angela Roquet** is a delightfully macabre weirdo. She lives in Missouri with her irresistible BFF husband, their sweet, clever son, and a majestic marshmallow of a Great Pyrenees in a house stuffed with books, toys, skulls, owls, and glitter-speckled craft supplies.

Angela is a member of the Science Fiction and Fantasy Writers Association, as well as the Four Horsemen of the Bookocalypse, her epic book critique group, where she's known as Death. When not swearing at the keyboard, she enjoys playing with her family and reading books that raise eyebrows.

You can find Angela online at **www.angelaroquet.com**

If you enjoyed this book, please leave a review or tell a friend. Your enthusiasm and support make these books possible, and it means the world to me!

www.ingramcontent.com/pod-product-compliance
Lightning Source LLC
Chambersburg PA
CBHW050841190726
48286CB00007B/2171